cop. 1

GILROY

FROM NOON TILL THREE

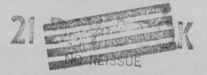

FROM NOON TILL THREE

BOOKS BY FRANK D. GILROY

Novel
PRIVATE

Plays
FAR ROCKAWAY (one act)
PRESENT TENSE (four one act plays)
THE ONLY GAME IN TOWN
THAT SUMMER—THAT FALL
THE SUBJECT WAS ROSES
WHO'LL SAVE THE PLOWBOY?

Children's Book
LITTLE EGO (with Ruth G. Gilroy)

FROM NOON TILL THREE

The Possibly True and Certainly Tragic
Story of an Outlaw and a Lady
Whose Love Knew No Bounds

FRANK D. GILROY

Doubleday & Company, Inc., Garden City, New York

1973

Cop./

ISBN: 0-385-08295-9
Library of Congress Catalog Card Number 73–82254
Copyright © 1973 by Frank D. Gilroy
All Rights Reserved
Printed in the United States of America
First Edition

For the same old bunch

FROM NOON TILL THREE

A Letter to the Editor

Gladstone City, Wyoming
September 7, 1881

Dear Sir,

I had just come back from feeding Belle and was tidying the living room—plumping up the blue velvet pillows on the divan, when I heard horses.

I looked out the window.

Five riders, two of them sharing one horse, were coming along the road to town. When they got to my path, they turned in and approached the house.

I am not a suspicious or timid person, but something about those men, even at a distance, stirred me with apprehension.

Living out here ten miles from town with no other houses between me and there, and Edna and Sam, the couple who work for me, being off for the day, was part of the reason for my anxiety but mainly it was the purposeful way they were coming up that path which their leisurely gait only seemed to emphasize.

They were in single file. The one later identified as the leader, Buck Bowers, close to sixty, white hair, a seamed and craggy face, led the way. Then came the Mexican who was singing a happy tune from his native land. Then the one with the scar who was called Ape for obvious reasons. And finally the horse bearing two riders: the one holding the reins a nondescript youth of nineteen called Boy who has never been further identified, and his passenger, Graham Dorsey, a thoughtful, brooding man close to forty.

There was some discussion outside the door that I couldn't hear and then a knock. My first reaction, which I obeyed, was not to answer. The knock was repeated—louder now. I stood there frozen. Then a voice, Buck Bowers's, not unkindly, said:

"We saw you at the window, ma'am."

I took a deep breath, assumed my most aristocratic and intimidating manner, and opened the door.

Buck Bowers removed his hat, signaled the others to do the same, which they did with ill-disguised reluctance.

My voice sounded higher than usual as I asked what they wanted.

"My colleagues and I are on our way to an important business meeting in Gladstone City," Buck Bowers said. "Unfortunately, that gentleman's horse"—he indicated Graham Dorsey—"broke its leg a few miles back and had to be destroyed."

"We need a horse," the one called Ape interjected impatiently. "You got any?"

Before I could respond, Buck Bowers inserted that they would pay a premium price.

My mind did a hasty calculation—concluded that if I

told them I had a horse (Belle—my beloved roan who was feeding at that very moment in the barn not fifty yards away) but didn't wish to sell her, the matter would not end there.

"I'm sorry I can't help you," I said, "but the fact is I don't have any horses for sale or otherwise."

"What's the barn for?" Ape sneered.

"Horses," I said, "but the couple who work for me have driven them to town for the day."

No sooner had I said this than there was a knocking sound from the barn which resembled nothing so much as a horse kicking its stall.

"What do you suppose that was?" Ape leered.

"*Caballo*," the Mexican said. "*Caballo*."

"We also keep cows there," I said. "It was a cow."

Graham Dorsey, without a word, dismounted and started toward the barn.

I pictured Belle eating away—realized what a fool I was to try and fool them—wondered what they'd do to me which was immediately answered by Ape:

"If he finds a horse in there, you're going to have to pay a little fine for your dishonesty," he said. His intention unmistakably lascivious was seconded by the Mexican who said something in Spanish that made me glad I had never learned that language.

I was trying to compose an alibi in my mind ("I was under the impression that Sam and Edna had taken both horses") and thinking what I would do next if that didn't work (jump back inside the house—bolt the door) when

Graham Dorsey who had disappeared into the barn now reappeared—was walking back to us.

"Well?" Ape called.

Graham Dorsey didn't answer till he reached us. Then he said, "There's no horse in the barn."

I almost gave the whole thing away right there, I was so surprised.

"Something kicked a stall," Ape said. "We all heard it."

"Like she said," Graham Dorsey told them, "it was a cow."

"There's not another place between here and town where we might get another horse, and we can't go in riding double," Buck Bowers said. "Looks like you miss this one, Graham."

"I hate to do that," Graham Dorsey said.

"I know," Buck Bowers said, "but that's the way it is. You wait here. We'll grab a horse on our way out of town and pick you up on the way back."

"Can we do it with just four?" the one called Boy asked.

"If I had any doubts, I'd call it off right now," Buck Bowers said.

"He don't get no share," Ape said, indicating Graham Dorsey.

"I'll divide it four ways," Buck Bowers said. "Those who want to give him something can."

My heart was slowing down to something approximating normal when there was that knocking from the barn again—more vigorous than before.

14

The Mexican rattled off an excited speech in his native tongue which Ape translated: "He says he never heard a cow kick a stall like that and neither did I."

"Are you saying I lied?" Graham Dorsey asked.

"I'm not saying nothing," Ape replied. "I'm just going down to that barn and have a peek on the chance you might have overlooked something."

Ape started to wheel his horse around in the direction of the barn when Graham Dorsey said: "If you take one step toward that barn, it will be the same as if you called me a liar."

The air crackling between them, they regarded each other.

Boy and the Mexican backed away conspicuously.

"I can take that bank with four men," Buck said, "but I can't do it with three."

The unruffled, matter-of-fact way he spoke defused the moment.

"We'll continue this conversation later," Ape said, jerked his horse around and started down the path toward the road followed by the Mexican and Boy.

"It's noon now," Buck said to Graham Dorsey. "If all goes well we should be back here by four o'clock."

"I'll keep my eye on her," Graham Dorsey said, indicating me.

"I'm sure you will," Buck said and spurred his horse to catch up to the others.

We watched till a bend in the road removed them from

sight, then turned to each other with an embarrassment as mutual as it was obvious.

He was, on closer inspection, taller than I thought (about six foot three) and, beneath the road dust that streaked his face, possessed a fine manly countenance that stopped short of handsome.

I don't know how long we might have gone on just standing there looking at each other if I hadn't thanked him for lying to the others about the horse.

"No man with an ounce of regard for women would have done less," he said with a drawl I hadn't noticed before in all the excitement.

"You're a Southerner," I said.

"And proud to be," he acknowledged.

He admired the house, said it reminded him of the many fine mansions, including his own, to be found in Atlanta before "that devil's march to the sea."

"I take it you were not always an outlaw," I said.

"You are correct," he said. "I was a colonel under General Lee's personal command. Rode with him from Bull Run to Appomattox. Returned to Atlanta to find my family slaughtered, my home and business destroyed. Catching one of the carpetbaggers in the act I shot him, was declared an outlaw, and thereby forced into my present way of life."

At the conclusion of this recital, he had a tear in his eye which I pretended not to see.

"Who dwells here besides you?" he asked.

"Just Edna and Sam who tend the place," I said, "and

they are off for the day—gone to town as I mentioned before."

"And your husband?" he said, regarding my wedding ring.

"Gone, too," I said.

"Where and for how long?" he asked.

"He passed away two years ago," I said.

He expressed his condolences—said he was sorry to do it, but that force of habit in the interest of self-preservation demanded that he go through the house to be sure I was alone.

I assured him, genuinely, that I was not offended and offered to lead the way, which he accepted with a bow.

We entered the house—me in front, him, hand resting lightly on his holstered gun, close behind.

In that fashion we proceeded through all the rooms on the first floor with him commenting knowledgeably on the furnishings.

In the kitchen he noticed the door to the basement—asked to be taken down there as well.

I lit a candle and preceded him down the stairs.

Casting eerie shadows on the wall, we moved through the cellar—had almost completed the inspection when there was an explosion in the corner.

In a single sweep he knocked the candle from my hand —closed his arm around me in a way that would have been scandalous if not for the circumstances, and simultaneously drew his gun.

The candle, still flickering, lay on the floor.

Silence for a moment and then Princess, the cat, emerged from the corner where the explosion took place, rubbed against my leg meowing softly while I explained to him that Sam made wine which he stored in that corner and that obviously Princess had knocked one of the bottles to the floor.

His breath warm against my neck (he was in a crouch) he inched us toward that corner where we found things just as I had surmised: a broken bottle and the odor of fermented contents from a puddle on the floor.

"You see?" I said.

"Yes," he said, but showed no tendency to relax his disconcerting grip.

"I would appreciate it if you'd release me now," I said as glacially as possible.

He hesitated till I was about to repeat the request, then as though he had suddenly wakened to the situation, abruptly let me go.

"My apologies," he said. "In the dark, your perfume and all, I was transported to another time and someone I held dear."

I suggested we resume our tour of the house.

Things proceeded without incident as we passed from room to room on the second floor.

Then we came to the closed double doors leading to the master bedroom.

"I would prefer you did not go in there," I said.

"Why is that?" he asked.

"Personal reasons," I said.

"What sort of a room is it?" he asked.

"A bedroom," I said, feeling like a ninny because I knew my cheeks were turning red. "I give you my solemn word there's no one in there or anyplace else in the house for that matter."

"I don't doubt your word," he said, "but if I didn't see for myself I would be unable to relax and the time we must spend together would be the less pleasant for it."

With that he tried the door. Finding it locked, he asked me for the key. When I offered no response he said it would be a shame to damage such a fine hand-carved door as that—raised his leg to kick.

I handed him the key which he inserted—turned.

The door swung open.

Gun in hand, he motioned me to enter first—followed on my heels.

We stood motionless, just inside the door, our eyes adjusting to the shadowed room lit by a single shaft of light that managed to evade the heavy drapes covering the windows.

Satisfied there was no one there, he moved to the windows—opened the drapes, flooding the room with sunshine.

His eyes went right to the great canopied bed and Otto's

nightshirt and robe laid out on the right side of the quilted spread—and, on the floor directly below, Otto's slippers.

His voice noticeably chilly and suspicious, he asked who those garments belonged to.

"Mr. Starbuck," I said.

"Who's Mr. Starbuck?" he asked.

"My husband," I said.

"I thought you said he passed away," he said.

"He did," I said.

"Then why are his things laid out like that?" he asked.

"Mr. Starbuck died of a heart attack on his way back from town one evening," I said. "His things are lying there just as they were that night. They have not, and never will be, disturbed."

"How can you sleep in that bed without disturbing them?" he asked.

"I haven't slept in that bed since the day it happened," I said. "I sleep in a room on the third floor. Now if you don't mind, I would like to discontinue this conversation which reminds me of that tragic event and upsets me greatly."

"If you don't like to be reminded of it, why do you keep this room like a museum and hide yourself away in the attic?" he asked.

"I consider your question impertinent," I said and started out of the room when he seized my arm.

"A beautiful woman locked away here in the bloom of her life—it's a crime against nature," he said.

"What has become of the Southern gentleman who prided himself on his sense of chivalry?" I asked.

"The first law of chivalry is to save damsels in distress," he said. "And I have never met a damsel more in distress than you."

"I appreciate your concern," I said, "but it is misdirected. My life is a happy one and very pleasing to me."

"Then why are you crying?" he asked.

Before I could muster a reply he was embracing me.

Taken by surprise, it took me a moment and all the strength I could summon to break away. Spent by the effort I collapsed to the floor beside Otto's slippers.

"I'm sorry," he said—sincerely distressed by my condition. "Can I get you anything?"

I started to say no when I remembered something.

"I feel a bit faint," I said. "You might fetch me some brandy from the dining room."

As soon as he left, I rushed to the closet, reached back on the top shelf under a blanket and drew forth Otto's revolver which was so heavy it required both hands to lift.

Cocking the hammer as Otto had taught me, I took up a position just behind the door and waited.

He re-entered the room bearing the brandy decanter and two glasses on a tray—did a slow turn until he was facing me.

"Glad to see you're feeling better," he said.

"Put your hands up," I said—training the barrel on his middle as Otto had advised.

Setting the tray down, he began to pour as though nothing had changed in his absence.

"Say when," he said.

"If you don't put your hands up, I will pull this trigger," I said.

"I'll take my chances that either the gun is not loaded or that you don't have the heart to shoot," he said, and having poured a sufficient quantity into one glass, now began to fill the other.

Sighting just as Otto had taught me and squeezing the trigger with the steady even pressure he recommended, I shot the glass out of his hand, which was as much of a surprise to me as to him since I was aiming at the floor.

His hands went up immediately and he regarded me with new respect.

"Beauty and spirit," he said. "Your husband was a lucky man."

Looking as firm and collected as I could manage, I directed him to unbuckle his gun belt, drop it to the floor, and kick it over to me. All of which he did.

"Sit there," I said, indicating the rocker in the corner, "and keep your hands on your head."

He moved dutifully to the rocker—sat with hands on head as requested—regarded me like an eager pupil who couldn't wait to see what delightful game the teacher would concoct next.

That unconcerned, almost blissful look of his, plus the fact he was rocking back and forth, disconcerted me more than anything that had happened so far.

"*Stop rocking,*" I commanded, which he did. Then, determined to erase his carefree expression, I said, "You are in very serious trouble."

"What do you intend to do with me?" he asked.

I had my plan all made but I told him I hadn't decided yet. I took a seat in the center of the room, the gun resting on my lap aimed square at him.

"We will remain like this until I've decided on a course of action," I said. "If you move so much as a hair without permission I will shoot."

"I believe you," he said, but his face never lost that blithe, unsettling aspect.

While I, of necessity, was compelled to regard him every second, he was free to look around wherever he wanted. But he didn't. He just kept staring at me.

I stood it as long as I could.

"If you expect me to be made so uncomfortable by your gaze that I will turn away and give you the chance to get the upper hand, you are in for a big disappointment," I said.

"I had no such intention," he said.

"Then why are you staring at me?" I asked.

"Because you said you'd shoot if I moved so much as a hair," he said.

"That doesn't include your eyes," I said. "You may look anywhere you wish."

"Thank you," he said, and continued to regard me exactly as before.

"You are still staring at me," I said.

"You said I could look anywhere I wished," he said.

"Anywhere but at *me*," I said.

"As you like," he said, and his gaze commenced a dutiful tour of the room.

"There's a crack in the ceiling that should be attended to," he said.

I thanked him for calling it to my attention.

"It's a long time since I've slept in a fine bed like that," he said. "Is it as comfortable as it looks?"

I did not reply.

"That kindly white-haired gentleman in the picture on the mantelpiece," he said, "is that your father?"

I must have betrayed some reaction, because he said, "Did I say something wrong?"

"The gentleman you're referring to," I said, "is Mr. Starbuck—my late husband."

"I'm sorry," he said. "My eyes are not what they used to be. From this distance I took him to be a man in his sixties."

"He was forty-five when he died," I lied—wondering why I felt the need to do so and hating myself for it.

"My eyes must be worse than I thought," he said, studying the picture.

"The authorities will provide you with glasses when you get to prison," I said.

"Have you figured out yet how to get me from here to there?" he asked.

"No," I said, "but I'm thinking about it."

"It must be going on to twelve-thirty," he said. "They'll

be back here by four and I'd hate to see them find us like this. It would be terribly embarrassing for me and highly dangerous for you."

"I appreciate your concern," I said, "but have no fear—I'll think of a plan in time."

"You know what I think?" he said.

"No," I said. "And I don't care to."

"I think you already *have* a plan," he said. "I think that you're expecting company. I think you expect a knock on the door at any moment and are just play-acting with me till they get here."

"Think what you wish," I said with an airiness that registered false even in my own ears.

"I don't *think*—I *know*," he said. "And I'll tell you *how* I know. You're blushing. Your cheeks are beet red."

He was looking right in my eyes again—so sure and knowing that I felt powerless to order him to look elsewhere. Equally unable to sustain his gaze, I glanced away and was instantly tumbling in the air as he jerked the rug from under my chair.

I landed one place and the gun landed another.

Before I could recover he was upon me—his hands roaming my body outrageously.

"What are you doing?" I said.

"Searching to make sure you have no other weapons," he said.

I was willing to abide this but when I felt his tongue in my left ear, I knew he had more than security in mind.

25

Spurred by his touch, his tongue, I somehow managed to get away—ran from the room with him in pursuit.

He caught up to me halfway down the corridor; spun me about; embraced me.

Again I broke free. Got as far as the end of the hall when he caught me again—visited another unwanted embrace upon me.

Gasping for breath, I escaped his hold once more and was dragging myself up the stairs to the third floor when I realized it was all a tactic to wear me down to the point of exhaustion and helplessness.

Immediately, I stopped fleeing—looked back down the stairs at him with all the dignity I could assemble with a shoe missing, hair every which way and my dress torn:

"Very well," I said. "If you are so depraved that you would inflict your desires on an unwilling body then proceed."

Whereupon I sat on the stairs determined not to move a muscle no matter what.

For a moment he just regarded me so that I was beginning to think my speech had brought him to his senses. Then he scooped me up, carried me back to the master bedroom and deposited me on the quilt in the midst of Otto's things.

"I will not react," I vowed to myself. "No matter what he does I will not stir."

Closing my eyes, I imagined I was a corpse.

I had heard of men who enjoy making love to cadavers

and was beginning to suspect that he was one of them when there was a knock at the front door.

He desisted immediately—whispered that if I made so much as a sound it would be the end of me and whoever was knocking.

"It's Reverend Cabot come to discuss the church social," I said. "If I don't go to the door he'll come in to see if anything's wrong."

"The instant he crosses the threshold he's a dead man," he said, reclaiming his gun from the floor and spinning the cylinder to emphasize the point.

I told him what a fine man the reverend was, that he had five small children, pleaded with him to let me go to the door and send him away on some pretext or other.

"You would signal him that you're in trouble," he accused.

I gave him my solemn word I wouldn't. He reminded me of the incident with Otto's gun.

"I hadn't given my word then," I said. "But now I do: I swear by all that's holy that if you allow me to go to the door I will send him away and return here without attempting to signal in any manner, shape, or form—so help me God."

The reverend knocked again more insistently. In another moment he would enter.

"Please," I begged. "I implore you."

"All right," he said, helping me to my feet, "but remember I'll be able to hear everything that's said from up here.

One false word or inflection and you have made five children fatherless."

As I descended the stairs I straightened my dress as best I could, ran my fingers through my hair, called out that I was coming.

About to open the door I glanced up at him, gun in hand, leaning against the bannister. Talk about gall: he smiled and blew me a kiss before withdrawing from sight.

The reverend's arm was raised to knock again when I opened the door.

"Good day, Mrs. Starbuck," he said.

"Good day, Reverend," I said.

"I was beginning to get worried about you," he said.

"I was lying down," I said. "The fact is I don't feel too well and I wonder if we might not put off our planning of the social to another time."

The reverend said that would be quite all right and asked if I'd like him to fetch the doctor.

I assured him that wasn't necessary and wishing me a speedy recovery he went off.

For an instant I was tempted to run after him, but the thought of his five children stopped me.

I waved as he climbed into his carriage and drove away —then closed the door and turned back into the house where God knows what ordeal awaited me.

Returning to the bedroom as I had promised, I found him, hands behind his head, fully clothed, lying on the bed staring at the canopy.

"The reverend is gone," I said.

He offered no reaction or acknowledgment of my presence—just kept on staring.

"If it is still your intention to take me against my will, I will disrobe in order not to ruin good clothes and, more importantly, to get this filthy business over as quickly as possible," I said.

"No," he said.

"You don't want me to disrobe?" I said.

"It isn't necessary," he said.

"I don't understand," I said.

"Nothing is going to happen to you," he said. "We're just going to sit here like this till the gang returns."

"You've had a change of heart," I said. "You've seen the light. Praise the Lord."

"I'm tempted to let you believe that," he said, "but the truth is not so laudable."

"I'm afraid I don't follow you," I said.

"Just as well," he said.

His jauntiness was vanished—replaced by a deep, all-pervading melancholy.

"Is it anything you would care to talk about?" I said.

"No," he said.

"Sharing troubles often lightens them," I said.

"It is not a fit topic for conversation with a person of

the opposite sex," he said, "or anyone else for that matter."

I assured him that coming from Boston and having been to Europe I was a sophisticated woman who would listen to whatever he might say without prejudice.

"Even if I wanted to tell you, I wouldn't know how to put it into words," he said.

"Try," I said. "Please."

"I can't get it up," he said.

"Pardon me?" I said.

"I am incapable of an erection," he said. "You know what an erection is?"

Somehow I managed to nod.

"You see," he said, "you're shocked. I knew I shouldn't have said anything."

I assured him that my reaction was reflexive, intended no censure, and begged him to go on.

He did: recounted how he had been unable to accomplish the sexual act since his wife died, seven years ago. Described in luminous detail the many and varied attempts he had made, all unsuccessful, to overcome his deficiency.

"A year ago I gave up," he said. "Resigned myself to the fact that I would spend the rest of my life as a eunuch. You know what that is?"

Feeling as though I hadn't breathed in hours and not trusting my voice, I nodded.

"A eunuch for the rest of my days," he said. "And then this afternoon we came to this house. You emerged and

I felt something stir in me I never thought would stir again."

Not knowing where else to look I just kept staring at him as this incredible recital poured forth like a long pent-up stream that has suddenly found an outlet.

"The look of you, the smell of you, the touch of you," he exclaimed. "I was aflame with desire. *Aflame!* . . . And then that reverend knocked at the door. You went to him. And now the miraculous moment, the last chance to redeem my manhood, is vanished—gone forever."

Weeping copiously he turned his head to the pillow.

It is a heart-rending thing to see such a fine figure of a man in every other respect reduced to such a state.

I ransacked my mind for words to console but before I could find any he leaped up from the bed, drew his gun, and put it to his temple with unmistakable intent.

Without thinking I grabbed his arm and was grappling to wrest the weapon away.

"*Let me end it,*" he said as we wrestled. "*It's the only way.*"

"*You must not give up,*" I panted.

We were rolling on the floor now—him trying to press the gun to his head, me fighting to prevent him.

You would think, given our respective sizes, that it would be no contest but my deep reverence for life invested me with a strength that was awesome.

Back and forth we tumbled. Now me on top. Now him.

Then, abruptly, he stopped struggling—regarded me with the most curious expression.

I thought for a moment that he might be undergoing a heart seizure.

"Are you all right?" I asked.

He nodded—signaled me to be quiet.

"What is it?" I whispered.

"I think it's coming back—that feeling I had before the minister knocked," he said in a voice as hushed and reverent as though we were in a cathedral.

"You see," I said. "You must never lose hope."

In what seemed like a single motion, he lifted me up, transferred me to the bed, and embraced me.

As his face descended to mine I wanted to turn away but could not bring myself to erase the radiant look from his visage.

The same reluctance to restore him to his previous condition (the gun against his forehead was still vivid in my mind) stopped me from objecting or resisting as he began to remove my clothes.

As he divested me of the last of my garments I regarded Otto's picture, wanted very badly to turn it to the wall but feared the interruption might be disastrous and kept my peace.

Now he removed his own clothes—revealing that the sensation he'd experienced as we wrestled for the gun was not a false alarm.

I will not attempt to describe what transpired during the next half hour except to say that a complete cure was affected.

I do not refrain from giving details out of any sense of modesty or wrongdoing but because I fear prurient minds would enlarge them till the true nature of what was going on, and my reason for setting it down for all the world to see, was lost or obscured.

The essential fact is that by whatever mysterious and divine way such things come to pass, and despite the much disputed meaning of the word, I knew, sometime during that half hour, that I was in love.

I was going to say "in love *again*" but it wouldn't be true because my fondest feelings for dear Otto never remotely resembled what I now felt for Graham Dorsey whose head was half dozing against my breast.

"Are you awake?" I asked.

"Uh-huh," he said.

"I am a forthright person," I said, "so I will say now that I think I am in love with you."

"I *know* I am in love with *you*," he said.

Huddling closer, we lay there, me stroking his head, in blissful silence till he got out of bed.

"Where are you going?" I asked.

"To get the brandy," he said, "so that we can celebrate our joy."

Will I ever forget the sight of him moving, just as God made him, through the rays of the afternoon sun to the table on which the decanter rested and returning with two glasses which we raised to each other in silent toast, drained without taking our eyes off each other, and then, at my lead, hurled into the fireplace?

"What time is it?" I asked.

He said he didn't have a watch.

I went to the bedroom entrance—peered at the hall clock.

"Five past one," I reported and taking Otto's jewel-studded gold watch from the bureau drawer I wound it and set it, and lay it on the stand beside the bed.

"That's a handsome timepiece," he said.

"It's yours," I said.

Instead of hemming and hawing that he couldn't accept it and my having to talk him into it as most men would have done, he simply thanked me, said it was a gift he would treasure, and examined it.

I had forgotten about the inscription on the back which he now read aloud:

"To our beloved President Otto Starbuck on the occasion of his retirement from the employees of the Gladstone City Lumber Company."

"I lied to you before," I said. "My late husband was sixty-eight when he died."

"How did you come to marry a man so much older?" he asked.

I told him of growing up in Boston in the impoverished branch of a well-to-do and prominent family.

"To have only a good name is worse than having no name at all," I said. "You are trained to do nothing but look down your nose at ninety-five percent of the human race, because their breeding is inferior to your own, while at the same time the five percent you might properly associate with look down their noses at you because your financial condition is a well-known secret. A fine home on Beacon Street and we went to bed hungry many a night because our exalted name would not allow us to ask for assistance."

Graham caressed me sympathetically—asked how I got from that situation to this.

I recounted the visit of Mr. Starbuck, a wealthy and recently widowed man, to Boston on business.

"We met at one of those innumerable afternoon teas which I never missed because they afforded a chance to appease my hunger with all the dainty sandwiches I could gobble down as discreetly as possible. I'm sure everyone but Mr. Starbuck, the only stranger in the room, knew what I was doing but pretended not to notice until he, Mr. Starbuck, in that loud voice that Western spaces seem to cultivate said:

" 'That's what I like to see—a girl with a hearty appetite.'

"All conversation ceased as everyone turned to regard me frozen at the buffet with one sandwich in my mouth and another in each hand.

" '*Don't be bashful, little girl,*' he bawled. '*Eat up!*'

"My mouth too full to speak, my throat too constricted to swallow, I just stood there until it was obvious that the earth, despite my fervent plea, would not open up and swallow me. Whereupon I dropped the sandwiches to the floor and fled out the door and down Beacon Street. Did not stop running till I came to the Common where I sat on a bench and wept and wept. I think I might have cried myself to death if Mr. Starbuck had not found me there.

"'It is no sin to be hungry or poor,' he said, 'but it *is* a sin to persist in that condition because of pride.'

"'What choice do I have other than to persist?' I asked.

"'You can marry me,' he said. 'I have a mansion in Wyoming that, like me, would be mighty glad for your company.'

"'But I don't love you,' I said, 'and doubt that I ever would.'

"'There are other things of equal or greater importance,' he said.

"I asked what they were.

"'Food,' he said. 'All the food you could ever want.'

"He laughed as he said this and I could not help laughing, too. I think it was that laugh, the first of many we shared, plus the fact I had never been West and had all sorts of romantic notions about what life out here would be like, none of them even remotely fulfilled until today, that ultimately won me. In any case, when he departed Boston for Gladstone City a month later, I, the new Mrs. Otto Starbuck, accompanied him."

During the latter stages of my narrative I observed Graham's reflection in the mirror opposite the bed. He looked troubled. I asked if he found my story unsettling.

"No," he said. "Not in the least."

"Then why is that sad expression returned to your face?" I asked.

"For two reasons," he said. "First, because the time is one-fifteen which means we have only two hours and forty-five minutes left."

"And the second reason?" I asked.

"I fear the miraculous cure you effected may have been temporary," he said.

I assured him that the restoration of his manhood was a permanent condition but he was not convinced.

"The proof of the pudding is in the eating," I said.

At this point I again, and for the same reason as before, draw a curtain over subsequent activity. Suffice to say that when we next looked at the watch it was twenty-five to two; I had been proved right beyond question about the lasting nature of the cure; and we were reconfirmed in our deep and tender regard for each other.

I *will* say, because it occasions the next episode in that idyllic interlude, that when we sat up to see what time it was our reflections in the mirror revealed us moist with perspiration, some of his road dust rubbed off on me, and both of us looking like tousled ragamuffins.

"I think a good scrubbing is in order for the two of us," he said.

"Come with me," I said and getting out of bed I donned Otto's robe.

"What do you have in mind?" he asked.

"Something you'll like," I said. "Come on."

He got out of bed reluctantly—started to dress.

"Just your trousers will do," I said.

He pulled on his pants—strapped on his gun belt and followed me downstairs and out the rear of the house like a petulant child.

"Where are we going?" he said.

"You'll see," I said and led him down the path over the small rise to the pond.

"It will be cold," he said.

"No," I said and slipping out of the robe I dove in to demonstrate. When I surfaced I told him it was warm as toast—called him a sissy when he hesitated.

That did it: Draping his gun belt over a branch, he removed his trousers and plunged in, surfacing almost instantly with a bellow of shock and betrayal as he hit the ice-cold spring-fed water.

Pursuing me across the pond with a powerful stroke he caught me as I was about to scramble onto the great rock that slopes to the water's edge.

Vowing the most awful revenge for my treachery he lifted me from the pond, deposited me on the smooth sun-baked surface of the huge stone.

Once again a prudent veil, of necessity, descends, and

it is some time later, ten to fifteen minutes as close as I can judge, the two of us side by side on the warming boulder staring at the sky as I resume.

—— 🐛 ——

We read shapes into the few clouds that drifted by, then gazed into the blue.

"Did you ever try to imagine what you would come to if you went up, and up, and up?" he said—told how as a child he used to lie on his back, just like we were doing, and let his mind ascend like an escaped balloon—occasionally attaining such heights that he did not think he would be able to come down—actually had the sensation of fighting his way back to earth.

"I do not like to discuss infinity," I said.

"Why?" he asked.

"Because I feel sufficiently insignificant as it is," I said.

"I, on the other hand, find it a great consolation that everything I've done good or bad, particularly the bad, is of no great consequence in the over-all scheme of things," he rejoined.

"Have you done so many bad things?" I asked.

"More than I care to remember," he said in a tone of sincere regret.

"Such as?" I asked.

"Do you really want to know?" he said.

"Yes," I said.

He reflected a moment, as though uncertain whether to tell me or not, then rattled off the names of a score of famous bank and train robberies.

"I thought the James brothers, the Daltons, and the Youngers did all those things," I said.

"That's what everybody thinks," he said. "But in reality it was us—the Buck Bowers Gang."

"I never heard of the Buck Bowers Gang until today," I said.

"Of course not," he said, "and do you know why?"

"Why?" I asked.

"Because Buck Bowers was farsighted enough to realize that the most publicized gangs are the shortest lived," he said. "Therefore we always pretend to be the Jameses, Daltons, or Youngers whenever we pull a job."

"That's very clever," I said.

"Yes," he said. "Today for instance I was to call Buck 'Jesse' and he was to hail me as 'Frank.' Sometimes we go so far as to give autographs which is stretching things a bit since most of these famous fellows are illiterate."

"Have you no regret that they'll go down in history while you'll be unremembered?" I asked.

"Not in the least," he said and swore me to a solemn secrecy that I never would have violated if things had not turned out as they did.

Our hands unconsciously sought each other as we continued to lie there.

"This is the most perfect moment of my life," I said.

"Mine, too," he said.

"I would not mind dying at this instant," I said.

"Neither would I," he said.

"Suppose we did," I said. "Suppose you shot me and then shot yourself. What do you suppose people would think when they found us lying here with no clothes on?"

"Since I am an outlaw and you are a respectable lady they must conclude I raped you; that you got your hands on my gun and shot me; that I wrested the gun from you and killed you as I died."

"You're right," I said. "Any other interpretation would be unacceptable."

"Therefore, I suggest we go on living," he said. "Which I will not be able to do much longer if I don't get something to eat."

"When was it you ate last?" I asked.

"Dawn this morning," he replied.

"You poor man," I said. "Come with me."

We circled the pond to where my robe and his trousers lay; were donning those garments when he saw a large perfect sunflower leaning out over the water that he determined to pick for me. As he reached out to get it, his foot slipped on the mossy bank and he tumbled comically into the pond.

Me carrying the sunflower, and him carrying his gun belt, which he was not wearing when the mishap occurred, he followed me back to the house where I showed him Otto's wardrobe and invited him to exchange his dripping trousers for anything that caught his fancy while I prepared something to eat.

En route to the kitchen, I caught a glimpse of myself in the hall mirror—repaired immediately to my dressing room where I exchanged Otto's robe for a daringly cut red ball gown.

Moving swiftly to the kitchen I assembled a huge platter of leftover chicken and ham which I was depositing on the dining-room table, along with a bottle of rare wine Otto had reserved for a special occasion, when I heard him descend the stairs and call for me.

I directed him to the dining room and struck a pose calculated to increase his surprise at the sight of me in that gown.

The doors parted and his surprise was as nothing to mine: There he stood in Otto's full-dress suit—white tie, tails, the complete ensemble. The perfection of the fit was equally surprising. I had no idea Otto was that big.

We laughed till tears ran, then assumed our places with comic formality at either end of the great oak table.

He poured the wine with elaborate ceremony, and I pronounced a toast "to these several hours which have redeemed my life" which he said he couldn't hear because of the distance between us and moved to a place beside and at a right angle to me where our limbs could mingle intimately while above table we played at ladies and gentlemen.

My appetite, usually nil at midday, was considerable but no match for the prodigious amount he consumed.

When we concluded, we had emptied that wine bottle and most of another and, as he put it, "licked the platter clean."

I apologized for the undistinguished fare—told him I was a superb cook which I would have liked to demonstrate if we were not so pressed for time.

The mention of time caused him to look at Otto's watch, *his* watch now, and frown.

"What time is it?" I asked.

"A quarter to three," he said.

"Do you suppose we'll ever meet again?" I said.

"I would give anything to make it happen," he said, "but considering the circumstances, who can say."

That exchange, and our keen awareness that each passing second brought us closer to goodbye, made us silent and sad.

"This won't do!" he said, jumping to his feet. "We are wasting precious moments."

"You're right!" I said. "There will be time enough for melancholy later. Now, we must rejoice."

Taking him by the hand, I led him to the ballroom which had not been used since Otto's passing.

"Now what?" he said.

"We're going to dance," I said.

"Before the orchestra arrives?" he said.

"The orchestra *has* arrived," I said and uncovered the phonograph Otto brought back on his last trip to New York.

Graham had heard of such instruments but never seen

one and attended closely while I placed a cylinder on the machine, wound it up and lowered the needle.

Silence for a moment and then a Viennese waltz sounded through the room.

He might have stood there regarding the turning cylinder indefinitely if I had not offered myself to his arms.

He proved to be a proficient dancer.

As we whirled about the room, I closed my eyes, abandoned myself to his sure guidance.

The wine, the touch and smell of him, the sweeping circles we performed, combined to make me giddy. I had never fainted in my life but felt I was about to when he abruptly stopped dancing and embraced me.

I do not know precisely what thoughts led up to or preceded it, but suddenly I heard myself saying, "Why must we part? Why can't I go with you?"

He said I wouldn't survive a week of their way of life. I thought of the one called Ape and realized he was right.

"You could quit the gang—stay here," I said.

"You're forgetting I'm a wanted man," he said.

"We could live in Boston, Europe, anywhere in the world," I said.

"I have no money," he said.

"I do," I said. "Mr. Starbuck left me a wealthy woman."

"I could never allow a woman to support me," he said.

"It would only be temporary," I said, "a loan until you went into some business which I'm sure you'd succeed at whatever it was."

"There *is* a business I've always had a secret desire to be in," he allowed.

"What is it?" I asked.

"The banking business," he said.

I began to laugh till I realized he was serious.

"Before you rob a bank you study it carefully," he said. "Over the years I have become fascinated with banking procedure and the way it varies from one institution to another—have often dreamed of operating a bank that would utilize the best innovations and features I have encountered over the years."

"That dream is not beyond reach," I said. "It so happens that I have relatives in the highest banking circles in Boston."

"This is too good to be true," he said.

"I must warn you," I said, "that while they are the most prosperous members of the family, they are also the dullest."

"What an irony if the love you feel for me as an outlaw should vanish as I become a colorless financier," he said.

"I see a more serious threat to our relationship in the possibility that you will miss the gang and the excitement of your old way of life," I said.

"Anything is possible," he said, "but I am willing to take my chances."

"So am I," I said, and sealing our bargain with a kiss, we began to plan.

"It would never do to let the gang know what I was up to," he said. "Therefore, I will ride off with them as though nothing had happened and then, sometime later, when we are a sufficient distance from here, I'll leave them and return."

I confessed that the prospect of even so minor a separation pained me. He said it affected him the same way but that it had to be.

He looked at his watch.

"Three o'clock," he said.

"One hour left," I said.

"Just time enough to change my clothes and celebrate our union fittingly," he said, and scooping me up was heading for the stairs when we heard hoofbeats, a single rider coming hard from town.

Setting me down he went to a window.

"It's not one of the gang," he said.

I looked—saw a gray horse, a red-haired rider.

"It's Cody Taylor, a boy who lives on the next farm," I said.

"He seems in a terrible hurry," Graham said. "Go out and see what it's all about."

I fetched a coat to put over my ball gown, was starting to the door when Graham said, "He's slowing down. I think he's going to turn in here . . . *Yes*—he's coming to the door."

"What should I do?" I asked.

"Just act natural," he said and escorting me to the door took a position flat against the wall, gun in hand, while I braced myself as the hoofbeats neared and stopped.

A moment later, Cody was pounding excitedly on the

door and before I even had it open was pouring forth the awful account of death and destruction that attended the robbery of the Gladstone City National Bank by the Buck Bowers Gang.

I succeeded in calming him sufficiently to glean the following from his hysterical report:

By colossal mischance, the gang arrived at the bank only hours after the head teller was discovered missing with most of its assets.

When Buck Bowers announced it was a holdup, the townspeople, many of them ruined by the embezzlement, rose like a pack of enraged hornets.

Five townspeople and one of the outlaws (the Mexican) were killed in the savage battle that ensued. The other three members of the gang were captured, tried and found guilty on the spot, and were to be publicly hung at five P.M.—an hour and a half from now.

"I've never seen a hanging—have you?" Cody said, his eyes bulging at the prospect.

"No," I said.

"That's why I stopped," he said. "I'm on my way to fetch my folks and thought you might like to see it, too."

I thanked him for his thoughtfulness as he jumped back on his horse and galloped off.

Closing the door, I turned to Graham, who had heard everything, expecting to find him distraught and was surprised by the smile that greeted me.

"You don't look unhappy," I said.

"It's an ill wind that doesn't benefit someone," he said.

"I fail to see who benefits from this," I said.

"We do," he said. "You and I."

"How?" I asked.

"With the gang destroyed there is no reason for me to leave," he said.

Seeing that I did not share his joy, he asked what was wrong.

"I find it shocking that you can accept the plight of your comrades so lightly," I said.

"In the outlaw game you quickly learn to be realistic and not cry over spilled milk," he said.

"In this case the milk is not spilled yet," I said.

"I don't follow you," he said.

"They will not be hung till five o'clock," I reminded him. "There is still time for you to do something."

"Such as?" he said.

"I don't know," I said, "but surely you aren't going to let your friends die without raising a hand."

"Ape is an animal, the sooner dead the better," he said. "And the one called Boy I never laid eyes on till three days ago."

"But Buck Bowers," I said. "Surely you have some feeling for him."

"Yes," he said. "I do like Buck, but not enough to commit suicide for him—which is what I would be doing if I went anywhere near that town."

I was about to say how disappointed I was when I had an insight that explained everything:

"You're saying all this for my sake," I said.

"No," he said.

"Yes, you are," I said. "I see it clearly now. Your heart is breaking for Buck Bowers but you are denying your feelings out of love for me."

"You're right," he said. "I can't pretend any longer. If it wasn't for you I would try to save him regardless of the odds."

"You must do it in spite of me," I said.

"Why?" he asked.

"Because if you let him hang without doing anything you would regret it the rest of your life," I said. "Ultimately your guilt would come between us and destroy the blessed bond we now enjoy."

He argued that such a thing could never happen but I was adamant—told him that as much as I hated to see him exposed to danger I would not be his until he tried to save Buck and the others.

"There is little chance I'll succeed," he said.

"It's the effort that matters," I said.

"I have no horse," he said.

"You can use Belle," I said. "Now go quickly before I weaken."

After a final embrace that almost made me change my mind, he dashed to the barn and, moments later, was galloping down the road to town.

Just before rounding the bend that would remove him from sight, he waved. As I waved back I saw that in all the excitement he had neglected to change his clothes—was heading for Gladstone City in Otto's full dress suit.

I called but was too late. He had made the turn and was gone.

I stood there looking after him for a while then, weeping like a schoolgirl, went back inside.

I had it in mind to divert my thoughts and make the time pass by tidying up the house—was pondering where to start when a great wave of fatigue overwhelmed me.

Intending to take a brief nap I lay down on the living-room sofa and closed my eyes.

What seemed like seconds later I was awakened by a vigorous knocking at the door.

My first thought as I lay there trying to collect myself was that he had realized how he was dressed and come back to change. But then I became aware of how the sun had shifted against the wall and knew I had been sleeping for quite a while.

The knock was repeated louder than before.

Could it be Graham returned from his mission?

That happy thought sent me running to the front door which I flung open on a tableau I will never forget:

The sheriff and two dozen mounted men, several of them wounded, framing dear Belle across whose saddle Graham's body, the dress suit drenched with blood, dangled lifelessly.

The scream I emitted made the sheriff flinch and several of the horses rear up.

I started toward Belle but the sheriff restrained me.

"I do not advise you viewing the body any closer," he said. "We had to shoot him pretty thorough."

"Remove your hands from me," I commanded. I wish now that he hadn't but he released me at once and I went round to the other side of Belle, who nuzzled me familiarly as I passed, and saw just a glimpse of the little remaining of Graham's head, and Otto's watch dangling from his pocket, before I collapsed to the ground.

As merciful unconsciousness claimed me I sensed them crowding around looking down at me—heard one of them comment on the fact that I was wearing a ball gown which produced the last thing I heard—a snicker.

—— �», ——

When I came to, I was in bed with dear Edna and Sam attending me.

They told me I had been alternately delirious and unconscious for three days.

I asked what had happened in the interim.

They said the dead, both townspeople and outlaws, had been laid to rest.

I asked about "the one in the full dress suit."

They said he had been buried in Boot Hill along with the Mexican who was shot and the three who were hung.

"How exactly did he meet his end?" I asked—detecting a quaver in my voice despite my determination to exhibit no emotion.

They told how Ape, in an unsuccessful bid for clemency, had informed the sheriff that Graham was hiding out here holding me prisoner.

"The posse was on its way when they spotted him in Mr. Starbuck's fancy suit riding old Belle," Sam recounted. "They chased him for miles, lost him several times, but finally brought him down in what I understand was a fierce battle."

I asked how the town was reacting to the whole thing.

"You don't want to bother your head with any of that nonsense now," Edna said, smoothing my covers.

"That's right," Sam said. "The main thing you have to do now is rest and get your strength back."

"You are hiding something from me," I said. "What is it?"

Edna and Sam exchanged a look and then Edna broke down—began to sob.

It seems the gossipmongers were having a field day about Graham being found in Otto's dress suit and me in a ball gown—plus my reaction at the sight of his body.

"What are they saying?" I asked.

Edna and Sam hemmed and hawed until they realized I would settle for nothing short of a complete and candid report. At which point Sam excused himself on the pretext of some pressing chore and Edna, beside herself with embarrassment, said it was the general consensus in town that Graham (referred to as "that devil") had forced me, out of some perverse inclination, to wear the ball gown and done "God knows what" to me.

I asked what "God knows what" implied.

She took a deep breath, looked away, and mumbled something I didn't catch.

"Would you mind repeating that?" I said.

"*Rape*," she burst out. "*They think that devil raped you.*"

Resisting an urge to smile I asked what they, the townspeople, made of my collapse when I saw his body draped over Belle.

"They think it was because it brought back to you the hellish experience you had endured," Edna said.

"Then I have their sympathy," I said.

"No," she said.

"You mean they are *un*sympathetic to me?" I asked.

"Yes," she said.

"But why?" I asked.

"Because it is commonly held in these parts that a woman can only be raped if she allows herself to be," Edna said.

"Suppose the man has a gun?" I said. "Suppose he threatens to kill you if you don't submit?"

"It is commonly held in these parts that a virtuous woman would prefer death to rape," Edna said.

"Do *you* think I was raped? And if so, do you think less of me because of it?" I asked.

"Sam and I love you too much to either speculate or censure," she said and started to weep again.

"Enough sniveling," I commanded. "What I need is advice."

"Sam and I have discussed it thoroughly," Edna said, "and we think the best thing for you to do is move away."

"That would be an admission of guilt and wrongdoing which I will never concede," I said.

"Then you must deny anything happened," Edna said less hopefully. "If you proclaim it loud and long enough, perhaps the whole thing will die down."

"How do I account for the gown?" I asked.

"Say you were trying it on in anticipation of the Governor's Ball next month," she advised.

"And 'that devil' wearing Mr. Starbuck's dress suit?" I said.

"Say he put it on to make the others laugh," she said.

"And fainting when I saw his body?" I said. "How do I explain that?"

"Attribute it to your shock at viewing such a gory sight and relief at discovering your beloved horse was safe," she said.

Knowing that I could never bring myself to tarnish what I had experienced by lying, I told her I felt any attempt to rebut their gossip would only dignify *it* and diminish *me*.

"Therefore I will say *nothing*," I vowed. "Let them make what they will of my silence but from this moment forth I will not utter another word about what befell me. Now fetch me something to eat for I feel ravenous."

As might have been anticipated, my steadfast refusal to discuss the events of that day with the various callers (Reverend Cabot, newspaper reporters, so-called friends) who came to pry, created a vacuum which diseased imaginations were quick to fill.

Edna and Sam, who did the shopping, brought back shocking reports of what was being whispered, and occasionally shouted, in town.

The vilest rumor maintained that I had lain with the entire gang, including the Mexican.

"You *must* speak out," Edna said.

"Never," I said and announced I was going to town (my first public appearance) the following day.

They said I wasn't strong enough, pleaded with me not to go, but I would not be dissuaded.

Sam, at Edna's urging, volunteered to accompany me as he helped me into the carriage next morning—was obviously relieved when I refused his offer and set forth alone.

I had not gone too far when I received my first indication of what was to come: the Taylor family (father, mother, the two girls and Cody) passed me going in the other direction. I bid them good morning which they returned with stony silence except for Cody who started to wave which earned him a resounding slap from his father.

The closer I came to town, the more my courage and resolve diminished.

At the outskirts of town I paused—fought a decisive battle with the urge to turn and flee.

Then, head erect, the team moving at a pace calculated

to indicate a lack of concern, I proceeded down the main street of Gladstone City.

As I rode, looking to neither right nor left, I reviewed my carefully planned itinerary:

First to the post office where I could count on a cordial reception from Mr. Wall, the genial postmaster, whose late wife I had helped nurse during her final illness.

Then to the dry-goods store where I would place an order of sufficient magnitude to overcome any ill feeling the owners might harbor.

Finally, the railroad depot where I would ask Lem Wallace, who never failed to stutter and blush in my presence, about a nonexistent parcel I was expecting from New York.

Judging those three stops to be a sufficient showing of the flag, I would then depart the town as unhurriedly as I entered.

On subsequent visits I would gradually prolong my stays and increase the number of stores until I was fully re-established in my orbit.

That was the plan as I entered town.

This was the reality:

As I progressed along the street, I felt the world freezing in my wake. A quick glance over my shoulder confirmed it: men and women, mouths agape, looking after me like so many disapproving dummies.

Gradually, the silence behind me gave way to a sullen babble (too indistinct to be deciphered) which accompanied me all the way to the post office where I tethered the carriage and entered.

At my appearance, Mr. Wall, who was laughing about something, assumed a look of glacial rebuff that wounded me to the soul.

"What can I do for you?" he asked as though he'd never seen me before.

"Stamps," I said numbly. "I would like to purchase some stamps."

"We don't have any," he said.

"What sort of a post office is this?" I demanded—anger beginning to restore some sense of feeling.

"It's a post office of the United States of America founded on an uncompromising respect for God and country," he said and, putting up a GONE TO LUNCH sign, closed the window in my face.

Emerging from the post office, I encountered a growing and increasingly hostile crowd.

They parted a bit at my determined advance, but it still required some shoving and a few arch "Pardon me's" to reach the carriage.

It seemed prudent to skip the dry-goods store, but a stop at the railway depot was mandatory if I was to avoid leaving the impression they had chased me out of town.

With the crowd trooping after me, I proceeded at a determined gait to the depot where Deke Franklin, a chinless man I never liked, greeted me at the entrance wearing the stationmaster's uniform.

"May I help you?" he said, smiling venomously.

"I would like to speak to Lem Wallace," I said.

"She wants to speak to Lem Wallace," he told the crowd which prompted catcalls and jeers I ignored as best I could.

"Lem Wallace is gone, which is why I'm now the stationmaster," he announced.

Something told me to let it go at that and depart, but a curiosity I have never learned to control, plus a determination not to appear rushed made me ask what had become of him.

"She wants to know what's become of Lem Wallace," he called to the crowd.

A veritable chorus shouted *"Tell her!"*

Whereupon that ferret had the sadistic pleasure of informing me that Lem Wallace was one of the five courageous citizens killed by the Buck Bowers Gang.

A woman in the forefront of the crowd reviled me as cruel and heartless for not even knowing the names of the dead.

It was true!

Completely absorbed in my own grief over Graham Dorsey, I had never asked who the other victims were.

Unable to say anything that would excuse my apparent callousness, and moved by the memory of dear Lem Wallace, I wept.

"The more you cry, the less you pee," a raucous voice bawled and the crowd, echoing variations of that sentiment, closed around me ominously.

Engulfed by raging faces and clawing hands that now

assailed my person, I closed my eyes to suffer their wrath with as much dignity as possible.

They knocked the bonnet from my head. They stomped my feet. They scratched and spit upon my face. They ripped my dress.

All this activity seemed to inflame rather than spend their anger and I fear to think how it all might have ended if the fire bell had not rung.

"*The stable!*" someone shouted. "*The stable's burning!*"

My eyes squeezed shut, I felt them leave me with a rush. When I was sure they were gone, I looked.

Flames were licking the face of Ehrlick's Stable threatening all the stores at the far end of town.

In the ensuing excitement and confusion I managed to make my way to the carriage and escape without further notice.

Whipping the horses all the way, I made it back here in record time.

At my entrance, Edna nearly fainted.

Glimpsing myself in the mirror (bruised, tattered, bloody) I felt queasy, but knowing if I gave way Edna would follow suit, I said she was fired if she so much as shed a tear and ordered her to draw my bath.

The next day, when they felt I was sufficiently recovered from my ordeal, Edna and Sam solemnly presented themselves to announce that while they would continue to serve me gladly any place else in the world, they would not continue in my employ if I insisted on remaining here.

"Our decision is made out of concern for *your* safety as well as our own," Sam said.

"I know that," I said.

"Say you will leave," Edna pleaded.

"I want to," I said, "but I can't."

"Why?" they asked.

I longed to tell them what had transpired between Graham and I which invested the house with such glorious memories, and a sense of his presence, that would bind me to this place forever.

I did not tell them because I knew they would not really understand, and because I felt that even the *attempt* to share the experience would somehow diminish it.

And so, several days later, Edna and Sam, thinking it was twisted pride and obstinacy that caused me to remain, made their sorrowful departure.

I was alone now.

Cody, his father's objections overcome by the sizable tip I gave each time, did my shopping and some of the heavier chores.

People occasionally paused to regard the house, and some kids broke a few windows one night, but beyond that I was allowed to live peacefully so long as I didn't show my face in town where, according to Cody, feeling against me still ran high.

The days spent tending the house and grounds, the nights spent in sweet reminiscence, I might have lived out my life and taken my secret to the grave if a trip, under an assumed name, to a doctor in the next county had not confirmed my growing suspicion that the nausea and other irregularities I had been attributing to my emotional state were due in fact to being three months pregnant.

I experienced a moment of panic at this news which gave way almost immediately to a flood of joy for I knew with absolute certainty that it would be a boy and look exactly like Graham.

This happy thought sustained me, singing and laughing, all the way home, and it wasn't till I closed the door behind me that the serious problems I now faced began to surface.

En masse they loomed insurmountable so, in the hope of reducing them to manageable proportion, I listed them as they came to mind:

1   Need of local doctor since the one I saw today is too far away. Will Dr. Rainey treat me? Remind him of Hippocratic oath.

2   Reaction of townspeople to pregnancy. Keep secret as long as possible.

3 Who will help me as I become heavy with child?
4 Who will fetch doctor when time comes?
5 Will Reverend Cabot agree to baptize?
6 If child is treated with ridicule, scorn, and abuse, as I'm sure he will be, how do I cope?

Enumerating the above had the opposite effect to what was intended—plunged me into a severe depression that persisted till bedtime when, as I blew out the candle, the obvious solution to all my problems at a single stroke, which I had been resisting all afternoon, burst over me:

I would leave Gladstone City before the pregnancy was discovered! I would go to England—have my child delivered by doctors far superior to anyone in this area. I would reside in London in one of those beautiful houses I had so admired on my visit, dwell in an atmosphere of culture and civility sorely missed here.

Once having decided to leave, happy thoughts came tumbling:

The child's surname must, for propriety's sake, be Starbuck, but there was no reason why his given name could not be Graham.

He would be raised as a gentleman—receive a fine education which, coupled with the physical prowess and looks inherited from his father, would carry him to untold heights.

Bubbling with anticipation I could hardly wait for morning to start making preparations.

—— 🌺 ——

My goal was to separate myself from Gladstone City without arousing curiosity or suspicion.

To accomplish this, I decided on a "visit" to Boston from which I would never return.

Fortunately, most of the money Otto left was in a Boston bank. What was deposited in Gladstone City I would leave and have transferred later to support the impression that my decision not to return was arrived at spontaneously.

The biggest problem was the house. Left untended, it would fall into disrepair and invite vandalism. On the other hand, the thought of strangers moving among the blessed memories that filled these rooms was abhorrent. For a brief instant I entertained the notion of burning it to the ground, but the complications that might engender stopped me. Ultimately, I decided to close it now (Cody's father, for an exorbitant fee, agreed to keep an eye on it) and have it sold later when distance would have hopefully made the idea less painful.

Dear Belle I would ask Cody to care for and later give to him for his kindness.

I would take only essential items with me and have the remainder of my possessions forwarded later.

Since my mail consisted almost entirely of anonymous hate letters, there was no need to leave a forwarding address.

Finally I sent Cody to the depot to purchase a round-trip ticket to Boston with special emphasis on "round-trip."

—— 🐲 ——

The night before the morning I was to depart, I finished packing and was taking a final tour of the house, fixing each beloved detail forever in my mind, when I remembered that I had never visited Graham's grave and knew I must go there to say goodbye.

Saddling Belle for the last time, I headed for Gladstone City.

Except for two men in the midst of a drunken argument, who went by without noticing me behind some bushes at the side of the road, I encountered no one on the way to town which I reached about one A.M.

Moving carefully along the deserted streets I made my way to the unkempt area, reserved for outlaw and indigent dead, called Boot Hill.

Tying Belle to a tree I moved among the crude wooden crosses till I located one marked BUCK BOWERS, and next to him one lettered simply BOY (not wishing to disgrace his family he had refused to further identify himself), and finally came to the cross marking Graham's grave.

As strongly as I felt his presence in the house, it was infinitely stronger here.

After a moment to collect myself, I spoke the piece I had been preparing all the way to town:

"I have decided to leave Gladstone City, Graham, and am here to say farewell and explain the reasons which you might disapprove of if you didn't know. To make a long story short, I am pregnant and it is for the child's sake, to spare him the scorn and abuse that would be visited on him here, that I am leaving in the morning for Boston where I will stay a few weeks and then depart for England where I intend to reside permanently. To part from this place will pain me as much as it does you, but I'm sure you realize it's what I must do and wish me bon voyage."

No sooner had I concluded when there was a clap of thunder which, because the sky was cloudless, gave me pause.

"Do you approve of my decision, Graham?" I asked tremulously.

And now the more skeptical (among which I counted myself until that instant) will be inclined to scoff as I relate what happened next:

A bolt of lightning struck the ground not ten yards from where I was standing causing me to shut my eyes. When I reopened them, Graham's spectre, the dress suit cleaned and pressed, was standing beside his grave.

"So you're running away," he accused, giving me no time to recover from my shock.

I started to repeat my reasons for leaving but he cut me off. "I heard all that before," he said.

"Don't you think the boy, and I'm sure it will be a boy, is entitled to a safe and happy childhood which I can only guarantee by leaving?" I asked.

"It all depends on what you mean by 'safe and happy,'" he rejoined.

"I did not come here to engage in a philosophic debate," I said.

"I know," he said sarcastically. "Your sole interest is the boy's welfare."

"That happens to be true," I said.

"*That happens to be false,*" he shot back. "*If you leave, it will be to insure your own ease and comfort!*"

"I will not be spoken to that way," I said and would have departed but my legs were paralyzed, riveted there.

"We have certain powers," he explained. "Now listen carefully to what I say and I will release you to do as you please."

"Very well," I said. "I am listening."

He took a moment to formulate his thoughts and began:

"Taking the boy away and calling him Starbuck will undoubtedly provide him with a more harmonious and comfortable life, *but* at the same time you will be depriving him of something infinitely more precious—namely his true heritage, his real name, and, above all, the knowledge that he is the product of a love so pure, and brave, and true, as to make it unique throughout the universe."

His words sent tears coursing down my cheeks.

"What you say is true," I said, "but I have no alternative."

66

"You *do* have an alternative," he said, "providing you have the courage to exercise it."

"I will do anything," I vowed. "Tell me what to do."

"We are not permitted to direct the actions of the living," he said. "All we can do is hint in the hope it will inspire to the right decision."

"You are beginning to fade away," I observed.

"Yes," he said. "My time is almost up so I must give you your hint without further delay."

"I'm listening," I said.

"John, eight, thirty-two," he said.

"Pardon me," I said.

"John, eight, thirty-two," he repeated, his voice and apparition growing faint.

"Is that a biblical reference?" I asked.

"Yes," he said and vanished from sight.

Repeating "John, eight, thirty-two," over and over, I mounted Belle and sped for home.

Arriving at the house, I leaped from the saddle and raced to the living room where the Bible rested on a stand.

Breathlessly I turned the pages to John, eight. Fingers trembling, I traced the numbers to verse thirty-two:

"AND YE SHALL KNOW THE TRUTH, AND THE TRUTH SHALL MAKE YOU FREE."

My initial reaction was one of letdown for I found no indicated solution to my dilemma in those words.

Reasoning that Graham would not have gone to all that trouble for nothing, I read the passage again and again in an unsuccessful attempt to discover a buried meaning that applied to me, was about to give up when a veil lifted and the whole thing was miraculously clear.

Falling to my knees, I thanked the Lord and Graham and, moments later, began to write this letter (which I intend to publish in the Gladstone City *Gazette*) so that one and all may know what actually took place that day and make of it what you will.

Sincerely,
Amanda Starbuck

Publisher's First Note — 1973

Amanda Starbuck's letter appeared in the Gladstone City *Gazette* on September 12, 1881—four months to the day after the bloody event that precipitated it.

It is a matter of record that on the day it was published, she sat in her house, doors and windows locked, a gun in her lap, determined to sell her life, and the life of her unborn child, as dearly as possible to the angry mob she expected might descend.

Imagine her surprise when the townspeople, with that perversity of reaction that audacious acts occasionally inspire, recognized her outpouring as the sincere and courageous document it was and took her to their collective bosoms.

This did not happen immediately.

At first they were quite simply stunned. Then a grudging respect began to leak in. Then, little by little, as the letter drew wider and wider attention, they actively rallied to her defense.

It was Reverend Cabot who turned the tide decisively when, in a Sunday sermon, he noted there was another verse in John, eight that applied to this situation—namely John, eight, *seven.* And he quoted:

"HE THAT IS WITHOUT SIN AMONG YOU, LET HIM FIRST CAST A STONE AT HER."

The clerical seal of approval officially bestowed, the stampede to her side was on.

It appears to have been romantics, proving once again, if it needed proof, that all the world loves a lover, who led the way.

Within weeks, Amanda Starbuck and Graham Dorsey were being likened to Romeo and Juliet, Anthony and Cleopatra, Abelard and Heloise, et al.

This romantic aura apparently extended to the Buck Bowers Gang, who were elevated by Mrs. Starbuck's account from a sorry bunch of minor ruffians to a status only slightly less celebrated than the Jameses and Youngers.

Graham Dorsey, because he risked and lost his life in that quixotic effort to rescue his comrades, was (and I have the newspaper clipping before me) likened to Jesus, while Ape is seen as Judas Iscariot.

Mystics, seers, and clairvoyants descended in droves to quiz Mrs. Starbuck about Graham's materialization in the cemetery.

Newspapers and magazines throughout the world feasted on the story and sent reporters to Gladstone City in search for more.

Neighbors who so recently had shunned Mrs. Starbuck could not do enough as her pregnancy progressed. It was as though the town had a proprietary interest in the coming child which was understandable since all the publicity had put Gladstone City on the map.

An ad in the *Gazette* of that day announces that:

> Mr. Herman Taylor (father of Cody who rendered such valuable assistance to Mrs. Starbuck in her darkest hours) will conduct a tour to the Starbuck mansion, giving an authentic account of what took place. The tour leaves from the Gladstone City Hotel at ten each morning. Admission one dollar weekdays—a dollar fifty weekends.

> EXTRA ATTRACTION: For two dollars additional, you will be granted an audience with Cody himself who will recount things hitherto unknown.

Last but not least in all the hullabaloo was the song "Graham and Me" ("I loved Graham and he loved me, and we lived a lifetime from noon till three" et cetera) which swept the country at the time and has mercifully been forgotten since.

All these elements and more contributed to the frenzy of public interest that swirled about Amanda Starbuck as she grew larger and larger and finally, nine months from the day of conception, went into labor.

Judging by the *Gazette* photograph, half the town surrounded the mansion during her five hours of labor, and, according to the next day's report on the black-bordered front page, there was not a dry eye in the crowd after Dr. Rainey came to the door and said, "The mother is fine. The baby, a boy, is dead. I have done my best."

The baby was dead, but interest in Amanda Starbuck and Graham Dorsey remained very much alive—seemed to intensify as the child's death invested their story with a sorrowful dimension that sent Mr. Taylor's price to "two dollars weekdays and three on weekends."

There being no mention of a private audience with Cody in the new ad, I researched the matter and found a brief story noting that he, Cody, had left town—no reason or destination given. As far as I have been able to ascertain he was never seen or heard of again in Gladstone City.

Which brings us to June the twenty-seventh, 1882, a Tuesday, two and a half months after the baby's death.

On the afternoon of that day Mrs. Starbuck returned home from a tea at Reverend Cabot's house where her mood was judged cheerful, leading everyone to the happy conclusion she was fully recovered from the loss of the child.

This cheerful mood apparently endured, for Mr. Taylor, standing outside the entrance to the Starbuck property, in the midst of his "authentic account," when she arrived home, testified she smiled at him in passing, an event he marked because she normally treated him with unconcealed disdain.

At approximately ten P.M. that night, Mr. and Mrs. Joseph Drexel were passing the Starbuck mansion on their way back from visiting Mrs. Drexel's sister in the neighboring town of Overton.

Mrs. Drexel had just noted there was a light in Mrs. Starbuck's bedroom when they heard an explosion from within that sounded very much like a gunshot.

Mr. Drexel, a frail man in his seventies, reasoning he could be of little help in an emergency, raced for town where he located the sheriff, apparently with some difficulty, for it was after seven A.M. before the sheriff arrived at the mansion and found Amanda Starbuck, in the words of the coroner, "Dead from a self-inflicted gunshot wound —the gun from which the bullet was fired still in her hand."

The general consensus was that while Amanda Starbuck had displayed a happy face to the world, her heart grieved for Graham Dorsey and the child until she could bear no more.

And so what appeared to be the final curtain descended on the story of these star-crossed lovers and remained down for ninety years (till January tenth, 1973, to be exact) when Mrs. Benjamin Hartley, sixty-five, while cleaning the attic of an old house willed to her by a distant relative in Kansas City, came upon an ancient stenographic pad, its weathered pages filled with faded but legible symbols that she, once a secretary, recognized as belonging to the Pitman system (the shorthand method in vogue when she was a girl).

Bored with cleaning and curious to see how much of her

old skill she retained, she started to transcribe the aged notations.

"I began the exercise idly with no intention of doing more than a page or two," she recalls, "but was soon so caught up in the tale that unfolded that I did not leave the attic until I had transcribed the entire thing."

It was Mrs. Hartley's husband, George, a Western folklore buff versed in the story of Amanda Starbuck and Graham Dorsey, who brought the stenographic pad to our attention.

Judging by the heated outcry that has greeted our announced intention to publish this document, and its rumored contents, it is plain that the public does not welcome the challenging of cherished legends.

While we do not bow to the pressure of public sentiment, which would mean not publishing at all, we do respect that sentiment sufficiently to present what follows without judgment or prejudice.

The Publisher

What the Stenographic Pad Contained

(a verbatum transcription)

Never mind how I look, the blood or anything, Mr. Bernard Glass, you just take down every word, including what I'm saying now, exactly as I tell it or you're a dead man. Now read that back and it better be on the nose . . . That's good work, Mr. Glass, now make sure you keep it up because I'll be testing from time to time. Understand? . . . All right then, let's begin. My name is Graham Dorsey. That's right, Mr. Glass, Graham Dorsey, the same Graham Dorsey that has become so famous thanks to Amanda Starbuck . . . That's what everyone thinks, Mr. Glass, but as you can see I'm *not* dead, not yet anyway . . . All that and more will be explained in due course if you stop interrupting . . . The date is—what is today's date? . . . October the twenty-second, 1882. It is three o'clock in the afternoon of a raw cold day and I am sitting in the office of Mr. Bernard Glass, whose door advertises that he is an accountant and public stenographer, bleeding all over his lovely upholstery . . . That's very kind of you, Mr. Glass, but I don't really give a fuck if you mind or not. Read that back . . . just the last part where I say "fuck" . . . That's amazing you can get all that down with a few squiggles. Where was I? . . . Did I say what town it is? . . . This is El Paso, Texas . . . It's nothing—just a twinge. You got any booze on the premises? . . . That's very considerate of you, Mr. Glass, but something tells me that instead of going to the saloon you might be tempted to go to the sheriff and inform him that there's a crazy man with a gun bleeding to death in your office who thinks he's Graham Dorsey . . . I've lost my faith in promises, Mr. Glass, so let's keep things as they are . . . Fine. Well, I guess you could say the whole thing began with a bad dream I had the night before we were going to rob the Gladstone City National Bank. The now renowned Buck Bowers had studied the bank and said it would be a cinch, so there was very little of the jitters there usually was on the eve of a job. The Mexican made his potent chili, and Buck broke out some beer he'd picked up while scouting, and it was like a party except for Boy, who, this being his first stick-up, was understandably nervous despite Buck's assurance that it would be just like rolling off a log. You sure I'm not going too fast for you? . . . Well, about eleven or so we turned in on this grassy knoll. Buck, the Mex, and Ape were snoring away in minutes. I chatted with Boy, trying to ease his mind by recounting how scared I was the night before the first job I pulled. Apparently I succeeded for he, too, was soon sound asleep. I regarded the stars till I felt drowsy, then closed my eyes. I don't know how long I was asleep when I dreamed that Gladstone City was deserted when we rode in the next day. Not a person or animal in sight as we proceeded down

76

the main street to the bank. When we reached the bank, Buck and Ape and I went in while Boy watched the horses and stood guard outside as planned. Buck started to announce that "This is a holdup" when we realized that the bank, like the town, was empty. "There's something funny going on here," Buck said. I was about to suggest that we vamoose when Ape, who had gone behind one of the counters, reported that the drawers were teeming with cash. Buck and I took a look and it was true. There was more money than we ever thought existed, bulging from each teller's stand and to top it all the vault door was wide open exposing a giant stack of gold bullion bars. Ape let out a roar of delight and started throwing the bills, none of them less than a fifty, into the air in great handfuls. Buck told him to settle down and soon had us systematically transferring as many of the gold bars as we could manage to our saddlebags while the banknotes we stuffed into our shirts, trousers, boots and hats, so that when we exited from the bank we waddled like overweight scarecrows, barely able to mount our horses.

"Where do you suppose everyone in the town is?" Boy asked.

"Maybe there was an epidemic," Ape suggested.

No sooner had he spoken when, without a sound, rifle barrels poked out from each and every window on both sides of the street.

The others apparently noticed it at the same time I did because Ape said, "Oh, my God," the Mexican said, "*Carramba*," and Boy emitted a sob.

"Keep going just like nothing was wrong," Buck commanded in a whisper.

And so, not looking right or left or daring to breathe, we proceeded up the street as though we didn't have a care in the world, and had gone almost three-quarters of the distance to the end of town, with those guns following us every step of the way, and might have made it if Boy hadn't panicked and made a dash for it that broke the spell—triggering the guns. The horses weighed down by the gold bars—our movements hampered by the cash we were stuffed with, we put up a feeble fight. I saw Boy, Ape, the Mexican, and Buck cut down in that order and then, as all the guns focused on me and were about to fire, I awoke.

Shivering from the dream, I glanced about the knoll at Buck, Ape, the Mex, and Boy who, in sleep, looked just like corpses. Blaming the dream on the Mexican's chili, which had caused me discomfort in the past, I lay down and tried to fall asleep again. No dice. As soon as I closed my eyes I was back on that street with all those guns pointing at me ready to shoot. All night long I lay there tossing and turning and by morning was sure of two things: the job was doomed and I wasn't going to take part in it. Well, I knew that if I mentioned the dream it wouldn't have any effect except they would rag me about getting nervous in my old age. Incidentally, my age now is thirty-seven which means I was thirty-six at that time and not "close to forty" as Mrs. Starbuck has stated. Oh-oh . . . That damn pain again . . . No, I don't want a doctor. I just want you to

stop butting in. Where was I? . . . Yes, well, knowing
the dream wouldn't mean anything I tried to talk them out
of the job by saying I doubted there was enough in the
Gladstone City Bank to make it worth our while. Buck said
he figured on ten thousand at least, which killed that argument, and I now gave up the idea of talking them out of
going and concentrated on finding a way to avoid going
myself. A way which wouldn't arouse suspicion since anybody who pulls out of a job at the last minute without
good reason might very well be a double-crosser who has
tipped off the authorities. Sickness seemed the best way,
so when the others rose at dawn they found me already
up. I allowed I had a severe cramp in my gut which had
kept me awake all night. Buck said it was probably just
the Mex's chili and I laughed along with the others, satisfied that the foundation was laid on which I would build
by not having any breakfast and complaining that the ache
was growing as we rode until finally at some point before
we reached town I would roll off my horse in a faint and
they would have to go on without me.

I can't tell you how good that coffee looked and smelled
but I passed it up. Boy suggested the possibility that
maybe I wasn't well enough and we should postpone the
job but I pooh-poohed that and said I was sure I'd be better as the day wore on.

Where we were camped was about twelve miles from
Gladstone City which meant we could travel at a leisurely
gait that would get us there about two and save the horses
for the getaway run. We had done about a mile with me

clutching my stomach and wincing conspicuously every hundred yards or so. And then Providence in the form of a chuckhole intervened. Sampson, my horse, stepped into the hole and broke his leg. I truly loved that horse, so my sorrow as I pulled the trigger to put him out of his misery was sincere.

"What happens now?" Boy said.

"He rides double with you until we come to a mansion about a mile down the road," Buck said. "We'll get him a horse there."

And so, me behind Boy, we proceeded to the mansion where this woman, Mrs. Starbuck, came to the door with an accent and manner of speech that made it clear she was a lady and not from these parts.

Buck asked her about a horse and I said a prayer.

She said she didn't have any horses and I was starting to breathe a little when that mare kicked its stall.

Like she has written, I went to the barn to see and there was this dumb Belle (that's two words, the second one the animal's name) eating away.

I had neglected my stomach symptoms since Sampson broke his leg so all my eggs were in one basket and my heart in my mouth as I marched back to the house and said it was a cow. Which I had no sooner said when the stupid beast kicked the stall again and Ape and I were headed for a showdown till Buck cut us off.

Moments later they were riding off to Gladstone City and I felt this great weight lift plus a touch of sorrow for I was sure they were heading for their doom. Which might make you wonder why I didn't jump on that horse and take off in the opposite direction.

There were two reasons. First, because dreams don't always come true regardless of how certain we feel, and second, because I now took a real good look at Mrs. Starbuck and decided then and there to bed her before I left.

The newspapers, and magazines, and songs, and what have you, have worked overtime to give the impression that she was a raving beauty. While I don't want to go overboard in the other direction and give her less than her due I think the record should note that she was tall for a woman, close to five seven, plain faced, and slender to the point that some might classify as skinny.

Why then was I so attracted to her?

For one thing, we had been on the dodge for seven weeks and I hadn't had a woman in all that time except for a quick thing with a squaw in Albuquerque where we cured Boy of his virginity.

Then there is the partiality I have always had for tall slim gals.

And finally, most influential of all, she had a bearing and manners associated in my mind with kings and queens which gave her an air of being beyond reach that made me want to have her more than any woman I ever met in my life.

I was racking my brains for a way to achieve my goal short of rape, which I vowed to forgo except as a last resort, when she, thinking I'd done it to save her, thanked me for lying to the others about the horse.

Without a moment's hesitation, and drawing inspiration from God knows where, I said, in a drawl you could cut with a knife, that no gentleman would have done less.

The drawl, which rang false in my own ears, passed muster with her, and within moments I was established as a Southern gent, reduced from riches to outlawry by the fortunes of war, whom she could treat as an equal and at the same time feel sorry for.

Needless to say I was neither Southern nor a gentleman. Had been raised in the St. Ignatius Orphanage in New York till I was fourteen, at which time I ran away with the Fitch and Teasdale Circus with whom I traveled the country for three years working my way up to assistant to The Great Reeves, an alcoholic lion-tamer I often substituted for and might have succeeded if Mr. Teasdale, an insanely jealous man, had not caught me in bed with his wife and chased me through the streets of St. Louis till I lost him by hiding in the back of a wagon where, exhausted by the run, I fell asleep.

When I awoke, I found myself part of a wagon train, bound for California, which I remained with as far as Abilene, Texas, where Mr. Blount, the wagon master, had me jailed for the theft of seventy-five dollars from a man named Kowlaski or Kowalchick which proved to be the luckiest thing that ever happened to me because the wagon train was not a week out of Abilene when they were wiped out, every man, woman, and child, by Apaches.

When news of the massacre reached the jail I felt the rest of my life was a bonus and, vowing to make the most of it, I threw in with some fellow inmates who were planning a jail-break I had previously refused to take part in because it seemed too risky.

On June 27, 1864, a Thursday (I throw in all these names and dates so they may be checked to prove what I'm saying), the escape plan, which began with me rolling around the floor of my cell like I was in awful pain, was put into action. The details would take too long to tell but the result was that we got away, killing the sheriff and a deputy, and I was launched on the life of crime that brought me to that fateful day. Who's that knocking? . . . Don't answer it! . . . Tell him to slide the newspaper under the door— no, wait a minute. Here, give him this dollar and tell him to fetch a bottle of whiskey. Go on now and be careful not to signal him in any way because I'll be watching every inch of the way. *Go on* . . . Well done, now take a look at this thing before we start again and tell me if you think the bleeding is slowing down at all . . . I don't care how the sight affects you. Do it! . . . Well, Mr. Glass, what's your verdict? . . . You're lying, Mr. Glass. The fact is I'm bleeding to death before your very eyes and the only reason I wanted you to see it is so you can testify later that I knew I was a goner and therefore had no reason to tell anything but the truth. Now, where was I? . . . Right. The gang had ridden off and she was convinced I was a gentleman despite the fact that I kept forgetting my drawl and finally dropped it altogether which she attributed to my having lived among rough people and in the North so long.

What she has written about my searching the house to make sure she was alone, including my getting a good feel of her in the basement when the cat knocked over the wine bottle, is true.

In fact just about everything she wrote up to the time I nailed her, including the gun she pulled, and the chase around the house, and the minister knocking at the crucial moment, was accurate except for two things:

Number one, I did not "comment knowledgably on the furnishings," which is a subject I know nothing about. What I did do was praise them, which her ears took for being expert.

And number two, and I want you to write this in capital letters in longhand so there is no possibility of it being misunderstood: I HAVE *ALWAYS* BEEN ABLE TO GET IT UP. Underline *always*.

Pretending that I couldn't, that I was impotent, was just a clever tactic that I knew she wouldn't be able to resist especially when I aimed the gun at my head.

If there is anyone who retains doubts about that, I advise them to check with Rosita LaVerne who owns a fine house bearing her own name in Dodge City, Mary O'Malley proprietress of the famous Mirror Palace in Laredo, and others too numerous to mention who will give firsthand support to my contention that I have never had any problems whatsoever in that department, so help me God.

Which brings us to the hearts and flowers part where she and I are supposed to have fallen in love and reached a state of bliss unequaled in the history of mankind. Where the hell is that kid with the booze? . . . He better be.

Well, there's no point beating around the bush. All that crap she wrote about what happened is just that—crap. The truth pure and simple is that she proved to be a great lay and we fucked the afternoon away, period. Why are you looking at me like that, Mr. Glass? . . . Like you didn't believe me—like you thought I was lying just now . . . No, you don't. You think I lied, and you know something, Mr. Glass? . . . You're right. She was not a great lay. She was eager and all, not having had it for a couple of years and then only from a man old enough to be her grandfather, but she was unskilled so that everything I did was new to her and exciting which plus the fact I hadn't had a woman in quite awhile and the luxurious house made for a nice afternoon. Does that satisfy you, Mr. Glass? . . . You're lying, Mr. Glass. It doesn't satisfy you. Like all Jews you have a keen eye for the truth so I will no longer try to fool you. I will come right out and say it. Yes, Mr. Glass, it was the best time of my life. Are you happy now? . . . Since you Jews don't miss a trick and you are probably jumping to sentimental conclusions about the tears in my eyes, I would like you to know they have no connection with what has just been said but are entirely due to the god-awful pain I am experiencing from my wound which I will not be able to endure much longer if that kid doesn't get here soon . . .

Now, let's get something straight. Just because I enjoyed that afternoon doesn't mean I go along with her account of what took place. We did swim naked in the pond and make love on that big boulder, but all that stuff about lying side by side and gazing at the clouds while we talked about infinity is a product of her imagination. So is the part where she says I fell in the water while trying to pick a flower for her. Anybody who knows me will tell you what I'd think of a guy who gave anything to a woman, much less a flower.

I did fall in the pond with my pants on, but it was simply a slip.

Being wet, I did have to change and for a lark put on that dress suit which fit so perfect it caused her to say she hadn't realized her late husband was so big. I let it go at the time, but the truth is that she had an exaggerated notion of my height. I'm no midget as you can see, but at the same time I'm a good deal shorter, four inches to be exact, than the six foot three she has endowed me with.

I'm smiling now because I'm recalling her in that red ball gown and me in the dress suit which, as she has noted, made us laugh at the first sight of each other.

Also, as she has noted, we consumed a great deal of chicken, ham, and wine while our limbs "mingled intimately" beneath the table. That's the way she put it—"mingled intimately." I like that. Along with thoughts of the food and the wine and all it is starting to give me an erection which could mean I am not wounded as seriously as I think. On the other hand, I've often heard it said that that urge is the last thing to leave a man. Will that kid never get back? . . . No, I don't want to take a rest. Talking keeps my mind off the pain. Read back the last thing I said . . .

From the dining room we went to the ballroom and she put on the phonograph which I had never seen before so we could dance. They say love is blind and I believe it for she has written that I was a fine dancer which must have come as a great surprise to all the girls at The Mirror Palace and a dozen other places where my attempts at terpsichore never failed to produce bruised feet and great laughter.

I do not recall the details leading up to it that she relates but suddenly she's telling me about all the money she has and is painting a picture of the elegant existence we could have together if I gave up the outlaw life.

I raised a few objections so as not to seem too eager, but in truth I was sold from the start. I'd been on the run for twenty years and was beginning to feel the aches and pains. And what was I but a second-rate outlaw in a second-rate gang which is all the Buck Bowers Gang amounted to despite the cock-and-bull story I'd told her about our exploits.

When I felt I had objected enough I gave in and we began to plan a life together including me as a banker which I was not fooling about when I said I had some very good ideas which this pain in my side tells me I should not take time to go into now.

Well, just about then this kid Cody arrived with the news that, like I dreamed, the gang had come to grief and Buck, Ape, and Boy were going to be hung shortly.

Seeing a bright spot in this for myself, I made the mistake of showing it because she had this notion that outlaws were like Knights of the Round Table who came to each other's aid in times of stress regardless of the odds—which does not bear any similarity to the facts.

When I saw that I couldn't talk her out of this lofty ideal, and might upset the apple cart if I didn't honor it, I saddled Belle and headed for Gladstone City with the intention of hiding out till the hangings took place and then returning to the mansion with a tale of how I'd ridden as swiftly as I could but arrived there moments after the traps were sprung.

The best laid plans often go astray as they say and this proved to be one of them.

I was a mile from the house and about to turn off the road for a nice nap in the woods when I met the posse head on. I didn't know it was a posse and was thinking about brazening it out—palming myself off as an innocent stranger when I realized that not only was I mounted on a horse they might recognize, but in all the rush I had forgotten to change clothes and was still wearing that monkey suit—bow tie and all.

I don't recall if they started shooting before I wheeled Belle and dashed into the woods or vice versa. In any case, that's what happened and the chase was on.

Belle proved to be a speedy little thing and we gained on them going through the woods emerging on to a big open field a hundred yards in front of the nearest member of the posse which I judged to consist of about twenty men.

They wasted a lot of shots crossing that field but nothing came close as far as I could tell.

I picked up a path on the far side of the field that brought me to a shallow creek which I forded to a place on the opposite bank about twenty-five yards upstream where I thought a stone outcrop might hide my tracks but it didn't and the chase continued through underbrush, across a farm where I went by a man plowing who, seeing me in that dress suit, must have thought one of his scare-crows had come to life and then on to a road where I began to detect that what Belle had in speed she lacked in stamina and knew I would have to lose them pretty soon or I was a goner.

Turning a bend I came to a fork in the road which promised to divide the posse in two and was debating which fork to take when I had a better idea. Glancing back to make sure they were not yet in sight, I took neither fork but went right up the middle to some bushes behind which I dismounted and stroked Belle's frothing muzzle to keep her from giving us away while I watched the posse come to the fork, hesitate a moment while they tried unsuccessfully to decipher which way I'd gone, and then, splitting into two groups, gallop by me on either side.

Suspecting that it would probably not be too long before they discovered their error, I remounted and took off cross-country. Had gone about two miles when I reached the crest of a hill where I looked back and saw that, as I had predicted, the posse was reassembled and on my trail about a half mile away.

What would have happened with Belle wheezing the way she was, if I hadn't come upon Dr. Finger I don't like to think about.

But there he was, Dr. Hiram Finger, shaving in a clearing beside a wagon which bore a sign advertising him as *The world's most painless dental surgeon thanks to a new wonder gas.*

What he thought of a man in a full dress suit approaching him in the middle of a woods I never learned for inspiration seized me as soon as I gauged we were about the same size and before he could say hello I had my gun out and was ordering him to remove his clothes as quick as he could or he would never pull another tooth.

For a man close to sixty, he complied with amazing agility, and was down to his underwear, which I told him was far enough, while I was still removing my shirt which I told him to put on along with the rest of the dress suit as we executed a switch of garments in record time.

It crossed my mind that Dr. Finger was taking this whole thing with amazing calm which I chalked up to his being a professional man and thought no more of at the time.

"What is that over there?" I asked when the exchange of garments was completed.

As he turned to look in the direction I was pointing, I brought the barrel of my gun down smartly against his head. I was pretty sure the posse had never been close enough to distinguish my face or how old I was but even if they had, the blood streaming down Dr. Finger's unconscious forehead would make identification impossible for the time being.

Leading Belle to the center of the clearing where Dr. Finger lay, I tied the reins to his wrist and mounting the wagon behind the old swayback who pulled it I took off with all the speed I could urge upon the poor nag without killing it.

I had reached the top of a rise overlooking the clearing when I heard shots and looking down I witnessed what all the participants, and now all the books and magazines, have described as "the ferocious battle" that attended the capture of Graham Dorsey.

Bull shit! And make sure you underline that. I saw the whole thing from beginning to end. They must have seen Belle standing there grazing and decided to encircle the clearing which they did and then, at a shout by a bald-headed man who I took to be the sheriff, they began closing in. I don't know who fired first or why but I can tell you it wasn't Dr. Finger who never regained consciousness throughout the entire thing and couldn't have done so in any case because I'd left him everything but my gun.

For whatever reason that first shot was fired, it drew several answering shots from the other side of the shrinking circle. Those shots were in turn answered by others and so on till every man was blazing away.

How Belle managed to escape unscathed in that withering crossfire is a miracle, but Dr. Finger was not so lucky.

Inflamed by the casualties they had suffered as they closed in, six wounded, the posse wreaked vengeance upon the body of poor Dr. Finger, pumping him so full of lead that his mother could not have recognized him.

I did not stay around to witness the embarrassed huddle that must have taken place when they found that Dr. Finger had no gun and everyone swore, as they must have done, to forget the true story in favor of the heroic version that has become so popular.

It was with a light heart that I continued on my way intending to abandon Dr. Finger's wagon when I was a safe distance and return to Amanda Starbuck and the bright future that awaited me.

I had just passed a sign saying I was seven miles from a town called Gretna and was looking for a place to ditch the rig when I passed a farmhouse from which issued forth a man with a rifle which he aimed at my middle and said, "You have your nerve showing up in these parts again."

Not being anywhere near the fast draw all those stories have made me out, I tried to reason with him:

"I think there has been some mistake," I said.

"You're damn right," the man said. "And you're the one who made it, Dr. Finger."

I protested, to no avail, that I was not Dr. Finger, and an hour later was standing before a judge in Gretna, whose name escapes me but wore a patch over his left eye, charged with relieving people of genuine gold teeth and replacing them with fake ones while they were under the influence of the wonder gas.

You would not think that persons who had seen him as close-up as his victims must have seen Dr. Finger in order for him to do his dirty work would genuinely mistake a thirty-six-year-old man for a sixty-year-old one whom I resembled in no way except that I was wearing Dr. Finger's clothes, which I now realized why he was so willing to exchange for my dress suit.

Well, the upshot of the trial was that I was sentenced to a year and a half in the state prison, which was a cruel punishment to visit on the other inmates upon whom they made me practice dentistry which I could not refuse to do without revealing my true identity.

I had been in prison four months when Amanda Starbuck's letter was published in the Gladstone City *Gazette* and swept to national and then international prominence by an ever-surging tide of public interest.

It did not take long for her story to penetrate even prison walls where it was greeted with as much, if not more, enthusiasm than the general public showed.

Once I got over the jolt of hearing my real name bandied about I began to enjoy the whole thing. Got a special kick when some of the inmates boasted about having ridden with the now famous Buck Bowers Gang at one time or another, and described the heroic Graham Dorsey, sometimes in direct response to questions from me, in such glowing terms that I felt myself blush.

I did not waste my time in jail. When I wasn't pulling teeth, which I must say I became quite good at, I studied all the books on banking I could obtain in preparation for my future career. And also books on English and grammar since we would be traveling in high society and I did not want to embarrass her or make a fool of myself.

The authorities were so impressed by my industry that they reduced my sentence and I walked out of that prison a free man on April first, 1882, which date should have given me some hint of what was to come.

Oh my God . . . "Is something wrong?" You mean outside of the fact I'm in pain and dying? . . . Keep writing— that's what you can do. Where was I? . . . Just out of prison, right.

To insure against discovery, I made my way to Gladstone City in a roundabout way that took three weeks and allowed me time to grow a beard and exchange Dr. Finger's clothes for the garb of a skinny-dipping minister, collar and all, which I topped off with a pair of glasses that gave me an evangelical appearance that would have passed inspection anyplace.

Arriving in Gladstone City I had to put up at a rooming house because the hotel was filled with tourists come to see the enactment of the robbery, which took place once a week, and view the other points of related interest including the scaffold, a permanent landmark, where dummies bearing a terrifying likeness to Buck, Ape, and Boy stood with ropes about their necks waiting for the traps to spring.

I also had the curious experience of waiting in line at Boot Hill to view my own grave.

Still trying to settle on a plan that would prevent

Amanda from suffering a heart attack or giving the whole thing away by her reaction when she found out I was alive, I joined Mr. Taylor's tour to the mansion to get a better lay of the land.

Mr. Taylor was at the end of his spiel, about the sad loss of the baby, when Amanda returned home looking much better than I remembered her. I experienced a warm flush throughout my body at the thought of all the bliss that was so close at hand and knew that the time to act had come.

Slipping away from the group, which was large enough so my absence wasn't marked, I hid behind a tree until all the carriages were gone.

Then, making sure no one was in sight, I approached the house and the beginning of my new life with feelings that can be more easily imagined than described.

She appeared almost immediately in response to my knock and again I was struck by the change in her appearance. She had a sort of radiance which was especially surprising in view of the loss of the baby.

"Can I help you?" she asked in a polite but impersonal way that showed my disguise was a complete success.

Not wishing to play the big scene on her doorstep where someone passing might see her faint, I said that I had become separated from the tour which had left without me and could I trouble her for a glass of water before beginning the walk back to town.

Ushering me into the house she invited me to have a seat while she went for the water.

I spent the time in her absence wondering how to break the news with a minimum of shock, and decided a gradual approach would be best.

"So this is where it all took place," I said as she returned, handing me a glass.

"Yes," she said.

"You must be sick to death of talking about it," I said.

"Not any more than *you* must be repeating *your* story," she said, and I nearly choked until I realized she was referring to my clerical outfit.

"Yes," I said. "I guess our situations are somewhat alike since we're both concerned with stories that have their roots in love."

"What a beautiful way of putting it," she said.

That seemed to break the ice and we chatted a bit during which I asked if she would ever consider marrying again.

"No," she said. "Once you have had the supreme experience others can only suffer by comparison."

"How true," I said. "How true."

"Being a man of the cloth, perhaps you would like to see the Bible in which I looked up John, eight, thirty-two."

"By all means," I said, and she led me to the living room and the stand on which the Bible was open to that page which she said she hadn't turned since the night she came back from the cemetery.

While I regarded the Bible, trying to think of a suitable comment, she stood at my side, the first woman I'd been that close to in a year, intoxicating me with her aroma and presence.

"That's what I call writing," I said, struggling not to blurt the whole thing out.

"Divine poetry," she said.

"Did you ever see it again?" I asked, uttering the first thing that came to mind while I searched for a short cut to the moment of revelation.

"It?" she said.

"The ghost of Graham Dorsey that you saw in the cemetery," I said.

"No," she said sadly. "I never encountered it again."

Tears welled in her eyes and I put my arm about her consolingly which seemed to calm her, but had the opposite effect on me.

"Suppose I told you that Graham Dorsey is still alive," I said.

"I know he is," she said. "In my heart he will never die."

"I mean *really* alive," I said, "living and breathing at this very moment."

"I didn't think Methodists went in for mumbo-jumbo," she said.

"It's not mumbo-jumbo," I said, removing my glasses. "Look carefully into my eyes and tell me what you see."

"You have green eyes," she said, giving no sign of the recognition I hoped for.

"I trust you have a strong heart, because you are about to get the shock of your life," I said.

"What do you mean?" she said.

97

"*I* am Graham Dorsey," I said, and was ready to catch her before she hit the floor which wasn't necessary because she just looked at me for a moment and then started to laugh.

"You don't believe it?" I said.

"No," she said and I could see she was trying to stop laughing the way you do when you think you're dealing with a nut.

"I know what it is—the beard," I said and made her accompany me to the bathroom where I had her stand with her back to me while I shaved my face clean with Otto's razor and then told her to turn around which she did with no change of expression.

"You still don't believe that I'm Graham Dorsey," I said.

"No," she said.

"Well, I am," I said and proceeded to tell her everything that had happened to me from the time I left the house that day right up to the present moment.

"Now do you believe me?" I said.

"No," she said.

"Why not?" I asked.

"For obvious reasons," she said.

"Which are?" I asked.

"You're sure you won't get mad if I tell you," she said.

"Yes," I said.

"Well, the fact of the matter is that Graham Dorsey was a lot taller than you for one thing and much better looking for another," she declared.

"Bull shit!" I said.

"And being a Southern gentleman he would never have used such language," she added.

"I am neither Southern nor a gentleman," I said.

"That's obvious," she said. "Now, if your pathetic little masquerade is concluded I suggest you leave."

I was at a real loss what to do next when I caught sight of myself in the mirror and knew what was wrong.

"It's this collar—these clothes," I said, and began to undress.

"Have you *no* decency?" she said.

"Relax," I said. "You won't be seeing anything you haven't seen before and might even recognize an old acquaintance."

Whereupon she bolted from the room and I, in my underwear, gave chase.

I tackled her at the entrance to the master bedroom where she put up a hell of a fight, but I finally pinned her to the floor and recited intimate details of our previous lovemaking which weren't mentioned in her letter-to-the-editor and therefore only she and Graham Dorsey could know.

She stopped struggling, looked at me hard for a moment and then said, "My God, it *is* you!"

"Yes, my darling," I said and planted a lot of kisses upon her face where they mixed with what I took to be the tears of joy she was shedding like a flood.

"*It can't be,*" she kept saying over and over, "*it can't be.*"

"It *is*, my dearest," I said and carried her to the master

bed where she continued to weep and wail while I undressed her.

"I know what it is," she said. "It's like the cemetery. You're a ghost."

"No," I said and, to prove the point, moved her hand to my privates which she squeezed until she was convinced I was flesh and blood, whereupon she sat upright and said, "*No!*"

"No what?" I asked.

"No lovemaking," she said.

"Why not?" I asked.

"Because I know that if we do, we will never be able to part again," she said.

"We don't have to part," I said. "We can go to Boston and all, like we planned."

"That was before when it was just the two of us," she said. "Now there are all the others to consider."

"What others?" I asked.

"All the people throughout the world who have been affected by our story," she said.

"Who gives a damn about them?" I said.

"I do," she said. "And so would you if you read some of the letters I have received from as far away as Japan saying how much my story, *our* story, has lifted their hearts."

"Three cheers for the Japanese," I said. "Now lie back down and let's get on with our reunion."

"Don't you see," she said. "We have become more than

ourselves and being more than ourselves we are obligated to subordinate our lesser selves to our greater selves."

"You must be talking Japanese," I said, "because I don't have the foggiest notion what you're saying."

"I am saying we must part," she said, "so that the legend of our love, which many people rank with Romeo and Juliet, may serve as an inspiration for generations to come."

"Look," I said as reasonably as possible, "I have been in prison for a year studying banking and grammar for when we go to Boston, and dreaming about nothing else but coming back here to you so much that I didn't even pause along the way to relieve myself because I didn't want to spoil my appetite and risk getting a disease, so stop all this about Romeo and Juliet and lie down and in ten minutes I guarantee you will forget about the Japanese."

"I'm sure I would," she said, "which is why I must cry a halt now before it is too late, for if people discovered I had taken up with another man it would be the end of our golden story."

"I am not 'another man,'" I said. "I happen to be Graham Dorsey and we are going to Boston."

"What would that gain us?" she asked.

"A happy life," I replied.

"What is a happy life in Boston in comparison to immortal fame," she said. "Do you know that at this very moment there are two stage plays celebrating our love running in Europe and an opera being prepared in New York. And this is only the beginning. Oh, Graham, Graham, turn your back on a few moments of earthly joy and, embracing the larger view, applaud me when I say we must part forever as though you'd never returned."

"And what do I do with the rest of my 'earthly moments' while you are polishing up our legend for eternity?" I asked.

"The outlaw game is in your blood," she said. "You must return to it until sooner or later you meet your Maker."

"What name do I use, since 'Graham Dorsey' now belongs to the ages?" I asked with a sarcasm that was evidently wasted on her, because she began to rattle off a raft of names I might choose from until I put my hand over her mouth and told her to listen:

"I am not going to outlaw again because I hate to outlaw," I said. "It's all saddle sores, bad food, filth, and rheumatism from sleeping on the ground. The Buck Bowers Gang was a penny-ante bunch who I rode with because I was no better than the others and if you don't take me to Boston I will reveal all I have said to the world."

"You would drag down your own name which is now spoken of in the same breath with Jesse James?" she said with amazement.

"Yes," I said, and she could see I meant it.

"They will hang you," she said.

"If they do I will at least have the satisfaction of spending eternity as my real self instead of Jesse, Frank, and the Youngers forever pointing me out as a fraud," I said. "No, by God, my name may be dirt but at least it is my name and I will not sacrifice it for false glory or anything else except going to Boston with you and becoming a banker."

"It will be your word against mine," she said. "I accept the challenge—now leave."

"I have no intention of leaving," I said. "I am going to stay right here and tell my version to all the sightseers Mr. Taylor brings out. Then you can tell your side and the people can vote on which one they believe. It should be quite a show."

"I believe this is called blackmail," she said.

"I believe you're right," I agreed.

"You win," she said, after a pause.

"What?" I said.

"You obviously have the upper hand," she said. "It would be futile to resist any longer."

"You're giving up?" I said.

"Yes," she said.

"You'll go to Boston like we planned."

"Yes."

"I don't believe you," I said. "You're doing it too easily."

"I have always been philosophic when it came to facing facts," she said, "and the fact here is that you've won, so why not make the best of it."

"I'm still not completely convinced," I said.

"Then perhaps this will do the job," she said, and putting her lips to mine gave me an embrace that went a long way to removing my doubts.

With a hunger befitting two people who haven't partaken of a morsel in a year, we kissed, licked and grappled, and were just about to begin the main course when she excused herself to answer a call of nature that wouldn't be denied.

While she was gone I thought of all the pleasures, immediate and future, that awaited me and was close to bursting with happiness by the time she re-entered the room and approached the bed in a slow way that seemed intended to tantalize, which it was doing, until she stopped just beyond reach and drew her hand from behind her back to reveal Otto's revolver which she aimed at my head.

"You will dress and leave this house immediately," she said coldly, "or I will pull this trigger."

"People will talk," I said.

"I will tell them you were a housebreaker who tried to assault me," she said. "Now get up and get dressed without making a false move or you're dead."

"You wouldn't shoot me," I said. "You couldn't. Not after all we've meant to each other."

"If you give me your word that you will never return and never reveal that Graham Dorsey isn't dead, I will see that you receive twenty-five dollars a week for the rest of your life," she said.

"That hurts me more than anything else you've said or done," I said and I meant it.

"Fifty dollars a week," she said.

"I love you," I said. "Can't you see that?"

"A hundred a week and that's my top offer," she said.

"I wouldn't care if it was a thousand," I said. "Nothing will make me get out of this bed until you return to it and say you're mine."

"You asked for it," she said and her finger started to lean against the trigger.

"*Wait!*" I said. "Before you do anything we will both regret, there is one thing you should know."

"What's that?" she said.

"It's important," I said, my mind racing in search of what to say next.

"Speak up or it dies with you," she said.

"Yes," I said. "Well, here it is. I have foreseen the possibility of this latest move on your part and so I left a sealed letter with a friend telling the whole story which will be opened at my death by this friend who along with other friends will confirm it by identifying my body as the real Graham Dorsey if you pull that trigger."

"You are bluffing," she said.

There comes a time in every man's life when he is faced with taking the big plunge or remaining a piker forever.

"Pull that trigger and see," I said, staking everything on one roll which for a terrible moment I thought I had lost because her finger was tightening on the trigger and, thinking I was a goner, I closed my eyes just before an explosion that rolled about the room and through my head in growing waves that convinced me I was dead until I peeked and saw her body on the floor.

My first thought was that she had fainted until I saw the blood beginning to puddle around her head and knew she had shot herself.

Do I have to tell you I was crying like a baby as I put out the lamp because I heard a carriage on the road, and regarded her lying there in a shaft of moonlight as though she were merely dozing.

"You have made a bad trade, my darling," I sobbed, "for I truly loved you and would have made you so happy in Boston."

How I dressed and got out of there I'll never know, but somehow I made my way back to the roominghouse in Gladstone City where the next day's paper carried a headline that said: OUR AMANDA TRAGIC SUICIDE— GRIEF FOR DORSEY AND BABY CAUSE.

I stayed around to attend her funeral which was almost more than I could bear—especially when they buried her side by side with my grave and enclosed us in a little white fence that kept us apart from the rest of Boot Hill.

Exchanging my clerical costume for the clothes and wallet of a salesman in the room next to mine, I departed Gladstone City determined to make the most of the new life she had given me and carry the secret she had died to preserve to my grave.

One of the new names she had suggested I might use was "Wild Dan Doby," which I liked except for the "Wild" which would never do for a banker, so I dropped it and presented myself as plain Dan Doby at The Citizens' Bank of Amarillo, where I informed the vice-president, a Mr. Blaine or Bane, that I was seeking employment.

"What experience have you had in banking?" he asked.

"None," I said, figuring honesty was the best policy since they would check any references, "but I am eager to learn and will take any position no matter how trivial in order to get started."

"I'm impressed by your enthusiasm," Mr. Blaine, or Bane, said, "but you are a bit too old for us to take on as a beginner."

Well, I guess I heard the same speech, or words to that effect, in a dozen different banks from Texas to Oregon.

I hadn't felt old at all when I started, but I can tell you that having a lot of people say you're old is a sure way to age a person in a hurry and by the time I was turned down in Oregon I knew I would have to give up becoming a banker or I would soon be ready for a wheelchair.

At a loss what to do next, I sat around my room drinking and discouraged until my eye lighted on the bag containing the tools of Dr. Finger's trade, which I had kept with me all this time and now knew why.

With a diploma, certifying I was a graduate of the New England School of Dentistry, manufactured by a printer in Virginia City, I hung out my shingle in Reno where I enjoyed a profitable practice until an unhappy customer checked on my credentials and had me run out of town.

When this same fate befell my efforts at dentistry for the third time, the last venture resulting in a near lynching, I saw the handwriting on the wall and turned my back on medicine forever.

There I was, Dan Doby, middle-aged and broke, a man with no past and even less of a future, while Graham Dorsey was growing in stature and popularity by leaps and bounds so that there wasn't a day I didn't encounter his name in some way including a stage play called *Graham and Amanda—A Tale of True Love*, which I attended and was asked to leave because all the falsity and tears it provoked in the audience made me stand up and boo.

Let me tell you what a torture it is to be feeling lower than a skunk's ass while your name is being praised to the sky.

Knowing you have pulled the wool over the world's eyes is no consolation if you're the only one who knows it, so I made my way to Laredo with the intention of visiting The Mirror Palace and sharing my secret with Mary O'Malley and a few other old friends who might put me in the way of a soft touch since it was clear that I would have to start outlawing again if I didn't want to starve.

Anticipating the delighted surprise with which she would greet my appearance, I entered The Mirror Palace and asking for Mary was directed to her private office which I entered without knocking.

"What do you want?" she asked, looking up from her desk.

"It's me," I said, "Graham Dorsey."

"Well, for crying out loud," she said. "How are you?"

"You don't seem very surprised that I'm not dead," I said.

"In this business you learn to take everything in stride," she said. "Do you still drink Bourbon?"

"Yes," I said.

"Good," she said. "Sit right where you are a minute and I'll fetch a bottle to celebrate your return."

"Don't mention to anyone else I'm here," I cautioned.

"My lips arc sealed," she said and stepped out of the room.

I was thinking about how good it felt to have someone know it was really you inside of your skin when the door opened and Mary reappeared with two muscular fellows whom she directed to teach me a lesson for daring to sully the name of Graham Dorsey by impersonating him.

"I *am* Graham Dorsey," I protested, as one of the fellows grabbed me from behind.

"Graham Dorsey was six feet four and as handsome and brave a man as ever lived," she said, with a tear in her eye. "If you are he, it should be no problem to get yourself out of this situation."

I was going to remind her of some of the great times we had had together when the fellow who wasn't choking me from behind sank his fist into my stomach which was the last thing I knew until I came to in an alley.

After washing the blood from my face where they had socked me, and straightening my attire as best I could, I limped over to the Roxy Stable, which was owned by Red Roxy with whom I had ridden on many a job in the old days before he realized there was more money in boarding horses than in stealing them and had gone more or less straight.

He was pitchforking hay into a stall when I appeared and damn near put the fork through his foot when I said I was Graham Dorsey.

"I can appreciate what a surprise it must be to know I'm not dead," I said.

"Yes," he said. "But it is a pleasant surprise because I had written off that fifty dollars as lost forever."

"What fifty dollars is that?" I asked.

"The fifty you borrowed from me in Dodge," he said.

"I don't recall that," I said, which was not so.

"Then you can't be Graham Dorsey," he said accusingly.

"You're right," I said and started away.

As I limped off I heard Red call to someone else that they just missed a good one because "some ugly runt was trying to pass himself off as Graham Dorsey."

And that's how it went with the other old friends and acquaintances I contacted who had all swallowed Amanda's story so completely that not one of them believed I was Graham Dorsey.

To make matters worse the outlaw game was in serious decline due to the spreading use of the telegraph which made escape harder, and the growth of railroads which were more difficult to rob than the stagecoaches they were rapidly replacing.

For a middle-aged man like myself the problem was especially bad because the few gangs still operating were, like the banks, only interested in younger men. So I was forced to go it alone robbing drunks, old ladies, and grocery stores, which added up to mighty lean pickings.

And all the time I was sinking lower and lower, he, Graham Dorsey, was going up and up till I expected to hear any day that they had made him a saint.

Graham Dorsey!

How I loathed that name which was depriving me of my very life and existence to the point that I had to pinch myself when I woke up every morning, and run to a mirror to make sure I was still there.

If I had to name the biggest aggravation of all it would be that goddam song "I Loved Graham and He Loved Me, and We Lived a Lifetime From Noon Till Three" which was played and sung in every saloon from border to border and was, therefore, a constant source of pain since I was spending more and more time in such places drinking larger and larger amounts to forget the wonderful life in Boston I had come so close to enjoying.

Which brings us to today and this fair city of El Paso where I was lapping it up in the Alhambra Bar and appreciating the afternoon quiet when a bunch of cowboys fresh off the trail came in to celebrate the occasion and were of no concern to me till one of them paid one of the girls to render his favorite song "Graham and Me," which so moved him that he began to cry and gave her a gold piece to sing it over, and over, and over.

If I had not had so much to drink I would simply have taken my business elsewhere but I knew I would fall on my face if I stood up, so I sat there with my hands over my ears which the cowboy who had made the request noticed and took objection to.

"I would not mind if it was just an insult to me," he said. "But I can't overlook an insult to the name of Graham Dorsey—as gallant a man as Texas ever knew."

I fully intended to apologize, but all the booze and months of suffering took over and I heard myself say:

"It might interest you to know that your hero, the great Graham Dorsey, was no bigger or better-looking than me, and no braver than me, which is to say he was a sidewinding faker and a shit."

"Give me room, boys," the cowboy said to his friends who were backing away before he even said it.

Then he approached the table where I was sitting till he was a few yards away and said, "Fill your hand, mister."

Not being quick with a gun, I had learned to be crafty which did not desert me as drunk as I was and so I had my gun out under the table where he couldn't see and caught him just above the belt buckle as he started to draw.

It was like a war after that with his friends all shooting and people running every whichway.

I believe I dropped a couple of them, including the girl who had been singing, before I got hit and passed out.

When I opened my eyes I was staring at a ceiling in what turned out to be the office of a doctor whose name I didn't catch who was standing off to one side telling some other people that it would be a waste of time to operate since I was a sure goner if he ever saw one.

I closed my eyes and remained so till they went into the next room and then got up and sneaked out the back with only one thought—to tell my side of the story and set the record straight before I kicked off, which brought me to this office because I had noticed your sign on the way into town. What is all that commotion in the street? . . . How did they know I was here? . . . Well, it doesn't matter. Nothing matters any more except that I pray to God you will see that my story gets into the right hands which should pay you more than enough to compensate for your time and the blood all over your furniture . . . Yes, there is one thing. Would you remove my boots before you let them in . . . You can stop writing now, Mr. Glass, for I am through.

Publisher's Second Note — 1973

In a postscript (also in Pitman) attached to the fore-going by Mr. Bernard Glass, he records that the man who had been dictating died just as he opened the door to ad-mit the sheriff and others who had been alerted to his whereabouts by the fresh bloodstains on the dollar bill which the newsboy presented at the saloon, plus the fact that everyone knows Jews don't drink.

"I told them that the dead man claimed to be Graham Dorsey and had dictated an impressive story to support his contention," Mr. Glass wrote. "But they ridiculed me and said if I knew what was good for me I would keep such nonsense to myself or people would think I was cuckoo and might even take offense."

"Being a Jew at any time, any place is hard enough," Mr. Glass concludes, "but in El Paso it is a supreme test, which is why I am filing this notebook away till the climate be-comes suitable enough to make its contents known."

Apparently the climate did not improve sufficiently dur-ing Mr. Glass's lifetime and the notebook passed un-noticed to his heirs when he died in El Paso in 1914.

How the notebook traveled from El Paso to the attic in Kansas City where Mrs. Hartley came upon it remains a mystery but in any case it ultimately arrived on my desk where I, disturbed by the recent spate of literary hoaxes, had it subjected to intensive chemical analysis which, in the words of the three experts who signed the report, "establishes beyond question that said notebook and the shorthand symbols therein are at least seventy-five and possibly as much as a hundred years old."

So much for the age of the document—what of its veracity?

Ninety years have all but obliterated the trail so that a team of investigators, while establishing certain facts (a St. Ignatius Orphanage burned to the gound with all records in 1900; a Fitch and Teasdale Circus; a wagon train led by a man named Blount wiped out by Apaches, et cetera) have been unable to prove beyond doubt that Dan Doby and Graham Dorsey were or were not one and the same person.

If they *were* one and the same person, then we have served the cause of truth.

If they were not, then we have presented a fiction which warrants no apology, for as my grandfather, who founded this firm, was fond of saying, "If you can't believe fiction, what *can* you believe."

The Publisher